ISBN 978-1-333-99465-5
PIBN 10218067

FB &c Ltd, Dalton House, 60 Windsor Avenue, London, SW19 2RR.
Company number 08720141. Registered in England and Wales.

For support please visit www.forgottenbooks.com

The Suburbans

By

T. W. H. Crosland

Author of

'Lovely Woman,' 'The Unspeakable Scot,' etc.

London

John Long

13 & 14 Norris Street, Haymarket

First published in 1905

CONTENTS

THE SUBURBANS

CHAPTER I

THEIR ORIGIN

ALL the world knows that the suburbans are a people to themselves. Persons of culture, of whom the more respectable quarter of the world is full, have for a generation or so made a point of speaking of the suburbans with hushed voices and a certain contempt. Among the superior class the very word 'suburban' nowadays means a great deal more than it was ever intended to mean. Indeed, though, philologically considered, it is quite an innocent word, with but one meaning, the superior mind has latterly contrived to pack into it meanings enough to start a respectable dictionary. To the superior mind, in fact, 'suburban' is a sort of label which may be properly applied to pretty well everything on the earth that is ill-conditioned, undesirable, and unholy. If a man or a woman have a fault of taste, of inclination, of temperament, of breeding, or even of manner, the superior mind proceeds, on little wings of haste, to pronounce that fault 'suburban.' The whole of the humdrum, platitudinous things of life, all matters and apparatus which, by reason of their frequency, have become somewhat of a bore to the superior person, are wholly and unmitigatedly suburban. It saves time so to dub them, and it soothes the weary heart. Omnibuses, for example, whether green, red, yellow, or otherwise, hurt in their lumbering vulgarity, not to say their utter disrespect for class distinction, every honest, superior soul. To ameliorate the average omnibus, to render it a vehicle of soft and spiritual delights, to rid it of its doubtful plushes, its uncleanly floor, its jogglety garden seats, its bloated driver, and its busybody conductor, were an impossibility. Five miles for twopence cannot be accomplished without certain inconveniently democratic concomitants. You cannot get, at a farthing a mile or under, the immaculate upholsterings, the soft cee-springs, the varnish, the exclusiveness, the obsequious touchings of the hat, which are yours by prescriptive right if you keep your own carriage. Hence it comes to pass that a bus, twopenny or penny, offends your delicate spirit, and in sheer unreason, when you ride upon such a rattletrap, you wax wroth and suffer the agonies of the tortured, and out of your martyrdom you cry: 'A plague upon omnibuses! They are suburban!'

Mutatis mutandis, it is so in a multitude of other concerns. Oyster-bars, Methodist chapels, free public libraries, small shops, ha'penny newspapers, cheap music-halls, police and county courts, billiard-matches, minor race-meetings, third-class railway-carriages, public museums, public baths, indifferent academies for young ladies: whatever, in short, strikes the superior mind as being deficient in completeness, excellence, and distinction may with absolute safety be called suburban. I am not aware that the theory hereby advanced does any real injustice to the suburbans. That they are, on the whole, a low and inferior species is proved by the fact that the name of them has furnished forth an adjective which finds general use when terms of contempt are required.

From the philosophic point of view, it is interesting to inquire how and in what manner the suburbans originated, and by what processes of decadence they have sunk to their present notorious abysses of ignominy. On the face of it, your true and unsophisticated suburban is a person who lives in a suburb. This may savour of Mr. Justice Blank's famous definition of a poet as a person who writes poetry; but it is nevertheless tenable and accurate. We may say with equal truth that 'in the beginning' the average suburb was essentially the offspring of snobbery. The prosperous urban who had lived over his shop for years finds himself, after much grubbing, so encumbered with superfluous wealth that he determines to acquire 'a sweetly pretty place a mile or two out.' To and from this rural retreat he drives daily in a gig. His wife and daughters learn to forget that they ever resided over a place of business. They wax stiff and exclusive, and the fresh air improves their complexions, taking the grease and the pallor from it. Other prosperous urbans note the change with envy and aspiration. They, too, will compass sweetly pretty places a mile or two out; they, too, will keep gigs; they, too, will improve the complexion, and incidentally the social status, of their wives and daughters by such a migration.

And here you have the first faint, tender shootings-up, as it were, of the suburb. If the site chosen by our adventurous gig-drivers has been propitious, all the rest follows. Clapham was started that way, so were Camden Town, Hampstead, Walthamstow, Highbury, Battersea, Tooting, and even that paradise of all that is suburban —Surbiton. It was the flourishing, superfatted shopkeepers who created the suburbs and the suburbans, and their work does them credit, and keeps green their memories to this day. For though they themselves, and their wives and daughters, and their gigs and sweetly pretty places, have long since disappeared, the spirit of them remains and abides, and is reflected in everything suburban; and will so remain and abide, and be so reflected throughout the centuries.

After the cits, of course, came the servants and bondslaves of cits—the clerks, the warehousemen, the bagmen, and general camp-followers of the cits—who in the course of years entirely overran the sweetly pretty places, and, encouraged by the land companies and the estate exploiters, gradually called into being their long, unlovely rows of semi-detached villas, their pinchbeck, unprepossessing High Streets, their flaring corner public-houses, their immaculate churches and young men's institutes, and their gaudy, blank-backed theatres.

It has been said that no man is to be blamed for his origins, and one may well wonder whether it is fair to consider the suburban as the creator of the suburb, or the suburb as the creator of the suburban. It seems probable that the more recent and latter-day suburban, with whom in this volume we shall have particularly to deal, is, in fact, the product of his suburb, and not in any real sense contributory to its rank suburbanness. So far is this the case that I believe it to be possible appreciably to modify and variegate the character and idiosyncrasies of any given suburban by setting him down in this or that particular suburb. I claim to be in a position to recognise the Hampstead woman, the lady from Lee or Lewisham, the man from Clapham, the gentleman from Surbiton, or the hobbledehoy from Bedford Park, at sight. They are each suburban to the marrow and all over them, but they have their differences, even as one star differeth from another. Moreover, I will undertake to make an entirely new spirit out of a Kensal Rise suburbanite by the simple process of committing it to a twelvemonth's residence in Bayswater or South Kensington. Indeed, the suburb has in effect so tremendous a power over the mind and heart of the suburban, that people born in Kilburn to the excellent and ancient patronymic of Solomons have been known on removal to Sydenham to blossom forth under the guise of Beresfords and Gordons. A suburb is a little thing, God wot, but it is as full of a certain starved kind of human nature as an egg is full of meat. To itself it is a whole cosmos, and, like the cosmos proper, it knows not where it began nor where it is likely to end. It has pride in itself, and faith; for you may sometimes hear a man from Ealing boasting that by bare virtue of his residence in that happy district he is a better, wiser, and sweeter creature than the man from West Ham. Of ancestry the suburban has uncommonly little to say. He is sensible that his family may be reckoned as new as his house. Long descent is not his vaunt. He prefers rather to swagger about locality. It is good that Heaven should have given him even so trivial a reason for self-satisfaction, inasmuch as his other reasons are slight and negligible in the extreme.

CHAPTER II

THEIR COUNTRY

GEOGRAPHICALLY considered, the country of Suburbia is prettily disposed in zones or rings. You have a big city, with the proper sections, commercial, residential, and fashionable, appertaining to a big city, and outside that—inexorably ringing it round—you have the eternal and entirely God-forsaken suburbs. Put together, they make the country which is the very saddest and most dreary and least delectable on all the maps. It is a country devoid of graciousness to a degree which appals. Deserts of sand, or alkali, or scrub were paradise by comparison. For it is a country wherein nothing is, save villas; where no bird sings excepting in front-windows; where the principal objects of cultivation are the stunted cabbage and the bedraggled geranium; where everybody's portion is soot and grime and slush; where the only streams are sewers, and the gardens are all black, and the principal population appears to consist of milkmen, postmen, bus-guards, scavengers, butchers' boys, nursemaids, drapers' assistants (male and female), policemen, railway-porters, Methodist ministers, and sluttish little girls who clean doorsteps.

Most other countries in the world have about them traces of the picturesque. Rural England boasts its pleasant lanes, its old-world villages, its ancient churches, and so forth. England of the cities, even if you visit the mirkiest of them, has invariably something to show you that is calculated to soothe or edify. London's bridges alone can offer you views which no man may gaze upon unmoved, and London has thoroughfares, and squares, and parks, not to mention cathedrals and other edifices, which are noble and elevating. In the provincial cities, from Edinburgh downwards, much beauty and much picturesqueness also exist. The very furnaces and factories and mills and foundries of the more industrial of them have a sort of rugged Cyclopean grandeur about them.

But in the country of the suburban these reliefs are utterly wanting. The nearest approach to them is furnished by a mammoth gas-holder or so, and by that couple of examples of flagrant, unblushing suburbanism, the Crystal and Alexandra Palaces. True, there are churches here as everywhere, yet ninety-nine per cent. of them are as new as pins and as ugly as brickyards. True, there are other buildings—assembly-rooms, music-halls, theatres, and the like—upon which the suburban is wont to plume himself. Yet in the whole arid area of Suburbia you shall not find a building that meets the eye graciously, or that does not bespeak a vile taste and a stingy purse.

It is on this matter of parsimoniousness that Suburbia at large seems to be based. Nobody in that country really wishes to pay for anything. On the other hand, everybody delights in cheap ostentation. Hence economy (save the mark!) coupled with flaring vulgarity is the keynote of the region. The one feature that takes the traveller's eye continuously, and perhaps not unpleasantly, is the public-houses. The miles and miles of villas with bay-windows and little back-yards to them, the rows on rows of indifferent shops where every article is marked on a basis of 'four-three,' the squads of dilapidated 'family residences' that have never been inhabited by a single family any time these fifty years, the hideous Board Schools, the still more hideous railway-stations, the idiotic free libraries—all these things fill the heart with sadness, and the mind with the bitterest reflections.

But the public-houses are distinctly and indubitably another pair of horses. I suppose that Suburbia's drink bill is in effect scandalously large. Your true suburban, of course, is most justly described as a moderate drinker. It is obvious, however, that this kind of drinker is precisely the kind of drinker whom the brewers, distillers, and publicans have reason to love. Taking him on the average, the excessive drinker consumes much less alcohol than his moderate colleague, though he makes more show with it. The moderate man drinks steadily year in and year out. The excessive man 'goes on the bend' only intermittently. There are both sorts in Suburbia, but the moderate man prevails, or at any rate he thinks he does.

It is the shining virtue of the drink trade that it looks well after its customers. 'You treat me decently, and I'll treat you handsomely,' is the workaday motto of his Imperial Majesty King Swipes. And in the matter of his suburban palaces, wherein he keeps revel and open house from six o'clock in the morning till half-past twelve o'clock next morning, there can be no doubt that he has been lavish and imperial. As mere buildings, these establishments stand out amid Suburbia's villas and cabbage-shops like oases in the desert. Architects of parts, builders whose name is not Jerry, reputable upholsterers and decorators, have clearly been employed in the erection and fitment of these mammoth houses. Costly marbles, honest building-stone, teak, oak, and mahogany of the soundest, fine plate-glass, solid brass and iron work, the chastest wall-coverings—these are the things that Swipes offers to his loving and bibulous subjects. Sometimes he rather overdoes it, but in the main he goes just far enough and no further.

Literally, the suburban public-house is the one thing about Suburbia which is eminently not suburban. That it should be so is, perhaps, a thousand pities. It makes the heart bleed when one reflects that in all this region of residences the finest, most palatial, and most artistic of houses are the public-houses. That the weary, soulless, overwrought denizens of villas, half-houses, maisonettes, cheap flats, and furnished apartments should resort to them assiduously for a little light and warmth and cheerfulness is not exactly astounding. They have their purpose; otherwise they would not exist. And who shall say that, all questions as to 'the stuff they sell' on one side, that purpose is not a benign purpose?

A further extraordinary trait of this country of Suburbia is that on all days except Sunday it is a country whose population consists almost wholly of women, children, and tax-gatherers. The true male suburban has to be up and out of Suburbia on the stroke of eight-thirty. The early backyard cock hath thrice done salutation to the morn. Therefore, Mr. Subub, wash your hands and face, put on your yesterday's shirt, swallow your tea and 'relish,' and proceed with all speed to your railway-station, or to your bus with four shining morning horses. All day shall you toil at your galley-slave's desk, what time the domesticities of Suburbia continue themselves without your aid or supervision. It is not until your return at night that your own country shall know you.

This absence of responsible male population throughout the day may be reckoned a much more serious matter than appears at first sight. It tends to render what is already suburban in essence more suburban still. Practically it gives over the household and all that dwell therein to the unquestioned rule of woman, which is not good. For a very large proportion of suburban housewives the daily round, the common task, does not really begin until within an hour or so of the blessed moment when 'he'—that is how Mrs. Subub invariably speaks of her better half—is expected to return.

In that hour all is bustle and excitement. The maids are adjured to activity because master is expected every minute. The Canterbury lamb is hustled into the oven without ceremony. Little Johnny is despatched to the corner shop for packets of desiccated soup and a penny egg for a custard. The dining-room is dusted swiftly with a tea-cloth, and the children's faces rendered free from marmalade with the help of mamma's apron. The parlour fire is persuaded to glow by dint of liberal applications of sugar and paraffin-oil. Papa's slippers are put to warm in the fender. Best of all, the next-door neighbour goes home to her own affairs.

When the gentleman of the house arrives he is usually grumpy. That upstart Jones has been browbeating him at the office. 'Nostrils' has gone down at Kempton Park, and the gentleman's week's lunch-money has gone with it. Or the train was fogged up for a whole twenty minutes; or he, the gentleman, has been put to the humiliation of a third-class stand-up journey because all the second-class compartments were choke-full, and the railway company has promised soundly to prosecute him if he ever again travels first-class with his second-class contract. He sinks into his well-cracked, saddle-bag, gent's arm-chair as one who has the cares of all the world upon him. He inquires why it is that 'the damned dinner' is never ready, despite the fact that there are three women in the house. He wants to know how many dozen pair of boots Georgie is going to use up next week. He is outraged at the sight of a final notice for rates which his good lady has pinned up over the mantelshelf for the pure purpose of jogging his memory. He pronounces the soup to be filth. The Canterbury lamb provokes him to remark that God made meat, and the devil made cooks. And, by the way, where is the beer? Why do women indulge such a contempt for one's little comforts? Hasn't he had a wicked day at the office? Is he a mere money-making machine, or what? The *Daily Telegraph* may well say that marriage is a failure. And so on and so forth.

This, of course, is all discipline for the household; it improves its tone and nerve and efficiency. But the fatal flaw in the system is the man's whole-day absence from his own domain. When the Underground and the bulgy buses have swallowed up their husbands, suburban wives take in deep breaths of freedom and content. By ten o'clock a.m. they are shaking dusters out of window and exchanging gossip, or renewing feuds over garden walls. Lunch in such houses is a Barmecide feast of cut-and-come-again from the ham-and-beef shop. Master is not at home, and consequently nothing matters. In the afternoon we slumber, or go to see our aunt, or our mother, or our newly-married sister, there to drink tea to repletion and to discuss 'him' and 'yours' to our feminine hearts' content. A strange country verily, and a pitiful people! Of its dead-level of dulness and weariness and meanness and hardupness who shall relieve it?

CHAPTER III

HOW TO GET THERE

MANY are the approaches to Suburbia. All roads, major and minor, lead thitherward. London's myriad omnibuses disject themselves upon that country day in and day out. If you descend into any one of her ten thousand railway-stations, you can get to the suburb of your choice for fourpence. Drivers of four-wheeled cabs will take you there for a moderate fare if you barter with them beforehand, or you can walk over the bridges and loll luxuriously in the electric yellow Marias provided by the London County Council or some such authority. Hereby, of course, rises up the grave question of locomotion. The male suburban population, with its pathetic complement of female suburban workers, must be carried to and from its tiresome place of residence somehow. The favourite facilities for such transport have been duly indicated above. Let us inquire into some of them more closely.

And first there is that fearful and wonderful hackney coach, the omnibus. You take an Elephant, and you change into an Angel, to quote the constable's advice to the old lady. Of nights and in the rain you struggle to the place where these buses stand. There is a pushful crowd of both sexes anxious to get home. Men and women cling to the rail and hop with one foot on the step in their desire to make sure of the coveted inside seats. They demand of one another in excited voices, 'Who are you shoving?' They exchange maledictions. The flounce of a skirt or so is rent audibly. The stout old gentleman from Putney barks his shins. An agile youth climbs on to the garden-seats by the outside of the stair. The conductor commands, 'A little sitting up on the right there, please.' The conductor's favourite fat passenger digs his umbrella vigorously into the bus floor, and remarks oracularly, 'Busy to-night.'

The conductor says 'Yas,' gives a jerk to the bell string, and we are off. The pace is that of the snail who has determined never to discommode himself by hurry. The seating accommodation, which looked soft and cosy, turns out to be hard and achey. You cannot move because of the fatness and elbowiness of that which is on either side of you. Your knees are jammed against other knees. You cannot converse, because suburban people seldom address one another until they have been introduced. You cannot read your greatly beloved pink paper, because the bus lamp flickers feebly and the roads are bumpy. Before you are gone one hundred yards a pert young lady out of a glove-shop remarks briskly, 'Conductor, please put me down at Cadogan Avenue.' With a pained look in his Cockney eyes, the conductor dives in among you for the fares. When you fumble for coppers, he glowers upon you impatiently. When you require change, he counts it out into your shaky hand, and tops it up with a threepenny-bit, wet and warm from his mouth. He punches the tickets with clangorous rings. In the middle of his collecting, maybe, the bus pulls up with a jerk, owing to some exigency of the traffic. Immediately the still, small voice of the glove-shop girl inquires if this is Cadogan Avenue. The conductor explains doggedly that he will 'not forget you, miss,' and, extricating himself from the jumble of knees, betakes himself nimbly to the charging of the outside passengers.

Meanwhile, dirty little boys take surreptitious draggly rides on the bottom step, and the fat old gentleman from Putney prods at their knuckles with the end of his umbrella. In the prolonged absence of the conductor the glove-shop young lady waxes anxious. Will anybody tell her 'if we have gone past Cadogan Avenue?' The conductor suddenly reappears. A stockbroker's clerk, whose hat has been ironed not wisely but too well, fixes him with an imperative stare, and says, 'Conductor, this young lady wants to get down at Cadogan Avenue, next turning to the Lord Derby.' 'Orlright, orlright,' sniffs the conductor wearily, and thus we progress.

By the time we reach our suburb, people begin

to drop off. Many of them descend 'while the vehicle is in motion,' for printed on the backs of the garden-seats upstairs there is a notice headed, 'We speak for those who cannot speak for themselves,' which every suburban has off by heart. It is a notice to the effect that passengers are requested not to stop the bus 'too frequently,' as the strain on the horses 'when restarting' is very great. Suburbia knows full well what will happen to it if it stops the bus too frequently. The conductor is sarcastic. He wants to know why you couldn't have got off at Lima Road, and whether you think you are 'riding on a bloomin' mowtor-car,' so that the youthful, and even the fairly middle-aged, prefer to take the risks. And now you are come into your suburb, with its cabbage and dried-fish stalls and their sputtering lights, with its shining grocers' shops, its yelling butchering establishments, its brilliant drink-palaces, and its innumerable dimly-lighted terraces, groves, and avenues all trailing away darkly into the night.

If you prefer the underground railways, there

is grime and heat and smell and rattle for you beyond endurance. When you have rushed headlong down a flight of stairs for the express purpose of catching the 6.45, the gate is banged rudely in your face by a grinning ticket-puncher. This, of course, is done to save your life, but it has an unedifying effect upon your temper. You argue excitedly with the ticket-puncher; you point out that the train you want is still standing in the station; but the gentleman with the nippers is adamant: he will not open that grimy wicket until your train has steamed off beyond recovery.

You 'wait for the next.' In five seconds a roaring monster comes out of the blackness. That is a Circle train. In another three minutes the joyous people who live at Hammersmith are accommodated. Then comes the turn of the Willesden folk. Then another Circle train, and so on. Your own drags in seven minutes late. You rush up and down it in the vain hope of finding a seat. By-and-by you are thrust desperately and by unknown hands into a compartment which is already packed with stand-ups. They resent you for the last straw. The more irascible of them would fling you out if they dared. The conversation of the remainder turns upon the wickedness of the railway company and the merits of a paper called the *Winning-Post*. All the way home you hang on by the sash-strap, inhaling a mixture of tunnel air, condensing steam, and rank tobacco, and wondering whether the man who invented underground railways did really bestow a blessing on the species.

Or it may be that the suburb of your heart lies somewhere in the delicate regions touched, served, and otherwise obliged, by that triumph of modern suburbanism, the Twopenny Tube. It is in this ghastly burrow that one becomes impressed with a proper sense of what the suburban, mightily assisted by his handmaiden Science, is likely to accomplish in God's world. The beginning of it all is a windy, encausticized passage, wherein you bang down twopence and put a pretty ticket into a glass box. Then a grille is swung aside, and you are ushered into a lift which glares with electricity, and is lined round with the advertisements of most things, from Parr's Pills to the *Saturday Review.* When a full load or complement of Twopenny Tubers has been secured by the stolid attendant, he shuts the grille with a rattle, turns a key, and down you go to the noise of humming-tops. At the bottom of the shaft you are set free to make your way through glazed passages to the platform. The air here catches you in blasts, and reminds you of charnel-houses and whited sepulchres warmed up. Till your train streaks in you are welcome to study more violent advertisements, red, yellow, blue, green, puce—all dazzling, and all jumping at you in the fierce electric light. In due time you hear afar off a rumbling murmur. Then, in the blackness of the tunnel at the end of the platform, you discern a moving light no bigger than a man's hand. The rumbling and the light draw nearer and nearer, and suddenly, with a rush and screech, the marvels of modern science have pulled up in front of you.

Men in uniform rasp back the iron wickets between the coaches, a few people step out, and you, for your part, step in. The wickets are clanged into their places, the conductors shut glass doors on you, and you may take your ease on a sofa-chair and breathe further unholy air. The journey is a journey which distresses you both physically and mentally. You rattle along through tunnels only just big enough to let your train through. At every station the attendant opens his glass doors, and rattles his iron wicket, and calls out the name of the station in more or less perfunctory accents.

You feel that, on the whole, it is not good for you to be there. The bowels of the earth, no matter how so well lighted, how so well tiled, and how so well ventilated, were never intended for the journeyings of mortal man, who, when all is said, is nothing if not a creature of the surface. And perhaps the most painful note of your trip is struck by the absolute complacency and unthinking satisfaction of these poor travellers under the sewers. At their music-halls and places of humorous entertainment they will hear 'the Chube' made the subject of many a merry jest, and they will smile. They will even joke about it themselves, and, if occasion arose, they would never hesitate to make complaints about it. But in their hearts they love and admire it. There is nothing under the sun so wonderful. Nothing in the world ever suited them more completely. Nothing has convinced them more surely of the tolerableness of life and the ultimate conveniences and glories which await patient Suburbia. The thought that it is not one man in a thousand who rebels and stands aghast at the whole business might move a stone image to tears.

On the whole, therefore, the ways into Suburbia are mean and squalid ways. There is little that is good to be said of them, and, if we except the Twopenny Tube, it requires every ounce of the suburban's philosophy to put up with them. The suburbans, need one say, do possess a philosophy of a kind. They have learnt it in a hard, meagre, unillumined school; but they bring it to bear upon the facts of life with a rough-and-ready cheerfulness which in a sense does them credit. To my mind, however, it is greatly to be regretted that they should have a philosophy at all. Indeed, for most men who are not excessively rich, philosophy is a snare and a delusion. There never was a philosophy yet—that is to say, a philosophy for poor men—that did not in the long-run teach that whatever is is best. It is this assumption which saps away the spirit and courage of the large mass of mankind. It is this assumption that makes Suburbia content, and even proud to be Suburbia. It is this assumption that has induced in the bosoms of the suburbans a sublime appreciation of red-brick villas, seven-guinea saddle-bag suites, ceraceous fruit in glass shades, pampas grass, hire-system gramophones, anecdotal oleographs, tinned soups, music in the parks, and kindred horrors.

Despite their peevishness and touchiness and want of conduct, despite their backbitings and slanderings and petty squabblings, despite their financial stringencies and the general narrowness of their affairs, domestic and otherwise, it cannot be denied that the suburbans do contrive to extract from life feelings of security, complacency, and completeness. For the individual suburban of our own time this is fortunate. For suburbans as a body and of future generations it is most unfortunate.

CHAPTER IV

THE MALE SUBURBAN

THERE is that about the male suburban which is calculated to make gods and little fishes laugh. It is wicked to laugh, of course, but in the circumstances who could resist it? For if there be a bundle of ludicrousness beneath the stars, surely it is the male suburban. The fact that he resides of nights and Sundays in a suburb is writ large all over him. A really decent man could live in a suburb twenty years without becoming in any sense the prey of the suburban spirit. I will not assert that the male suburban is other than a decent man; but he is also a man of whom the suburban spirit has obtained a complete and unqualified grip, and this is what distinguishes him from other men. You can tell the male suburban wherever you meet him. Consider him. Look at the unscrupulous respectability of him. Regard his well-brushed silk hat, his frock-coat with the pins in the edge of the lapel (they are always there) and the short sleeves, the trousers that are forever about to have a fringe on them, the cuffs with paper protectors and a pocket-handkerchief stuffed up one of them, the 'gamp' and its valuable case, the cheap ring, the boisterous watch-chain, the dainty side-whiskers, and the blue shaven jowl. The man's coats decline to sit properly on his back, because, truth to tell, he is all back; his trousers bag at the knees, because he is largely knees; and his boots burst at the sides, because he always buys them too small. If it were a case of neglect or scorn of appearances, the male suburban might conceivably be pardoned. But there is something in the preposterous air of the man which convinces you at sight that, so far from being a scorner of appearances, he is a zealous, assiduous, and never-flagging worshipper of them. He believes himself to be the glass of fashion and the mould of form. If he were otherwise, he thinks he might die. His tailor has guaranteed him 'West End cut and style.' Inside his twelve-and-sixpenny silk topper you may read 'Extra best quality,' and beneath, 'West End finish.' The fact that the whole contrivance might with accuracy be described as 'late property of a nobleman' does not occur to him. He is getting what he conceives to be the fashionable article on what he conceives to be economical terms. He is of opinion that he 'pays for dressing,' and his soul within him is glad. When that frock-coat shall grow shabby, he will have it bound with braid, though he would not take the pins out of the edge of the lapel for a fortune. When that hat waxes dinty and greasy, he will have it blocked and retrimmed; and when it gets past ironing and retrimming, he will buy something in a bottle wherewithal to rub and furbish it up.

All this, of course, shall be sworn by the unsophisticated to prove that the man is merely poor. I am quite open to agree that if he were a little richer he would go boldly into Bond Street and Piccadilly, and purchase himself attire of the radiantest. But I also know that his garments would be vulgar, and the effect of them disconcerting. I know, further, that he was the originator of, and is still a strenuous believer in, the axiom that a man should be judged by the clothes he wears, and that appearances must be kept up though the heavens fall. Here is his fallacy, and it is a suburban fallacy. No man above the degree of a fool ever took thought to put it into practice till suburbs began to be built. The sumptuary laws of Clapham, Balham, Ealing, Herne Hill, and Highgate—particularly Highgate—have decreed that the man who does not wear a silk hat and a frock-coat is hard-up, damned, and no gentleman. To be told that he is no gentleman breaks the male suburban's heart. So that he sticks to his extraordinary clothing like grim death, and, taking him on the whole, may be reckoned severer in such matters than Mayfair itself.

In every other respect the male suburban may be said simply to match himself. There is a dunness and a want of clarity about his complexion, even. It has a cast as of Clapham Common,

Wormwood Scrubs, or Battersea Park on it. In railway trains and on buses he is for ever paring his nails, and this especially of a morning. At nights and on the return journey he chews the toothpick which came into his possession at lunch, or smokes a carefully-preserved cigar. And, talking of lunch, there is probably no ghastlier feeding on the round globe than the lunch of the male suburban. Roughly, it is conceived in three principal types: 'Cut from the joint, two vegetables, bread, butter and cheese, one shilling'; or, 'Tea, scone, and apple dumpling, and talk to the neat-handed Phyllis, at an A.B.C. shop'; or, 'Welsh rarebit, canned salmon sandwich, and a glass of bitter, and talk to the neat-handed Phyllis in a saloon bar.'

All these things the male suburban calls lunch in good faith, and somehow he manages to get satisfaction out of them. Further, you shall perceive that, even though his feeding be as hurried as it is meagre, he is a great hand at table and bar manners. Always he goes for the salt with his knife—that is to say, if the bone spoon of gentility be missing. On occasions, when he happens to be flush of money, he will pay a penny for a serviette. He is a great consumer of mustard, because mustard imparts a recherchéness to pretty well everything, excepting, of course, apple dumpling, and it is not charged for in the bill, or 'ticket.' It is noticeable, too, that if a knife and fork are in question, the suburban sticks out the little finger of the fork-hand, and holds the knife-handle delicately between the thumb and the first finger of the knife-hand. If you ask him why he does these things, he will answer condescendingly: 'My dear boy, do you suppose we haven't been to school?'

Sometimes—probably three times a week on an average—my lord has a difference with the waiter. This, of course, is at the cut from the joint and two vegetable places; for a true gentleman never has differences with the young ladies who 'wait on' at A.B.C. shops. And touching the waiter who, good easy man, has charged our suburban with a penny for bread:

'George,' cries the suburban easily, after scanning his bill, 'what in the name of heaven is this?'

'A penny, sir—bread, sir,' replies George smartly.

'But I didn't have no bread.'

'Pardon me, sir, you did 'ave some bread.'

'Well, I say I didn't.'

'Can't 'elp that, sir. Bread you 'ad, and bread you're charged for.'

'Oh, well, I'm damned if I'll pay!'

The suburban has become furious. He threatens to call for the manager. 'Outrageous, abominable, scandalous—the idea, the idea! Do you think I want to buy the damned restaurant?' And then, in soothing accents: 'Now, George, I appeal to you, *as a man of the world*, would you like to be charged a penny for bread when you hadn't had any?'

George admits that 'it would be a bit thick,' picks up the gentleman's twopenny tip, and goes off to see if the 'boiled rabbit and pickled, two-in,' badly wanted at No. 7, has come up yet.

The male suburban saunters out, toothpick in

mouth, to his office, there to inform Spriggins, at the next desk, that he has just had a fine old row with that damned George at the Hen and Feathers.

'Beast wanted to charge me a penny for bread when I hadn't had no bread—but not for yours truly!' Doesn't Spriggins agree with him that this cursed tipping system ought to be abolished?

Spriggins says: 'Certainly, dear boy. What's more, I believe that if we wrote a letter about it to the *Daily Mail* they'd print it.'

'Good idea,' says the male suburban, and proceeds with the totting up of his master's figures.

It has been said by a more or less keen observer that suburban men are all clerks. This, of course, is not true, though on the face of it one would like it to be. But it is more than probable that seventy-five per cent. of the male denizens of Suburbia have some business in offices or other places of trade. On the other hand, there is probably not a suburb of any consequence in the Metropolitan area which cannot boast among its chiefest ornaments a fair sprinkling of professional people—solicitors, chartered accountants, auctioneers and valuers, Civil Servants, and last, but not least, in puffedupness, actors, authors, and journalists. These and the like of them are supposed to set the tone and standardize the manners and ambitions of the great mass of their fellow-dwellers in outward darkness. Probably they do so. But what a grubby, limited, old, unhappy, underbred crowd they are!

Without injustice to them, you may describe them as a mere projection of their own unholy, ill-paid, hungry, subservient, but nevertheless silk-hatted and frock-coated clerical assistants. Not to put too fine a point upon it, you shall find, if you scratch them, that they are just clerks with from thirty shillings to ten pounds a week extra income. And they swagger, and grumble, and gruntle, and wallow accordingly. The be-all and end-all of their lives is the main chance. They are the sons of generations of impecunious snobbery, and they grind, and sweat, and wrestle after halfpence, not because they care greatly for money, or pine for the leisure and ease which money can bring, but simply because they have got it into their savage hearts that life is a fight and a scuffle and a scramble, and that the keenest man wins—what time the devil takes the hindmost.

I am not disposed to deny them certain human qualities, though the suburban spirit has shapened even these into something which seems almost inhuman. There is many a petty advantage-snatcher in the City of London who believes himself to be an excellent husband and father, and who justifies his sharp practice and his wicked dealings, his sailings near the wind, his avarice and rapacity and cupidity, by the reflection that he is fighting the brave man's battle for his family.

'I have a wife: why should she not live at Rosebery House, and walk in silk attire, and outshine the neighbours, and give little dinner-parties? I love her, and it is my duty to keep the wind off her. I have sons and daughters, cheeky little snobs all, but they shall have education, education, education, and starts in life; for I love them, and I will work my fingers to the bone, and in some wise get the better of every soul I meet, to make little ladies and gentlemen of them. Furthermore, Johnny does me immense credit in his Eton suit and his real four-and-sixpenny college cap, and Gertrude is getting on admirably with her fiddling; and if that foolish girl Ethel would only pay a little more attention to her aitches, I think that young ass Schiffer might be got to marry her, especially if I put fifteen hundred of the best by the side of her.'

Indeed, life for this class of gentry is a plain matter of getting on, and continually getting on. To live at all, it is necessary to take incessant toll from other people—pettifogging toll if you will, but steady and progressive. And as it is all done for the perfectly honourable, legitimate and tender purpose of rendering the lots of Mrs. Subub and her dear chicks snug, comfortable, and independent, and impervious to the shocks of the world, I, Subub, shark, sweater, grabber, and pilferer though I may be, am still a good and comely man.

CHAPTER V

THE FEMALE SUBURBAN

For convenience' sake, and with a view more surely to impress the dense and torpid mind of the female suburban, I propose to cast this chapter in the form of a personal epistle, which, in my opinion, may be read by the ladies of all the suburbs with pleasure and profit. It may be pointed out, before going further, that the delineation of character hereby offered for nothing would cost at least a guinea in the psychological establishments of the West End, and could not be had for less than five shillings at a private séance in the cheapest suburb out of town.

Dear Madam,

I beg respectfully, and on all fours, so to

speak, to suggest to you that the fact that I should be compelled to call you a female suburban is neither your fault nor mine. You live in a suburb, and you are of the gentler sex; therefore, unfortunately, it is possible, and well within the limitations of the scheme of things, that you should be written down for a female suburban. It has been said, with great justice, that the hand that rocks the cradle rules the world. One may argue from that apothegm that the hand that rocks suburban cradles rules Suburbia. And, truth to tell, dear madam, this is again unfortunate for you. Inasmuch as, at time and time, I see a great deal of your male relatives, both in pursuit of their business avocations and in the cultivation of their small pleasures, it is only natural that I should hear somewhat of your fair self.

Usually, I may tell you offhand, it is the pleasing custom of the male suburban to refer to you either as 'the dear little woman' or 'the old girl.' I have also heard you called 'the enemy,' 'the missus,' and 'the partner of my joys and sorrows,' but this, of course, was by way of a joke.

Furthermore, it has been confided to me by gentlemen in various stages of emotional prostration that you are 'the best woman that ever stood on this footstool,' that there are 'no flies' on you, that you are a marvel in the cooking way, and that you never touch a drop—all of which is, if I may be allowed to say so, greatly to your credit. But, madam, the opinion of obviously and necessarily biassed persons does not matter, and the appearance and condition of those persons makes it quite evident that you are not by any means so white and pink as they in their gallantry would fain paint you. Without more ado, then, I shall venture the statement that, though he seldom owns to it, the male suburban is a hen-pecked, shrew-driven, neglected, heart-sick man. This does not reflect prettily on you, madam, but you must think about it and forgive me. Do you, on the whole, treat poor Charlie with the respect and deference due to his great position in the dissecting department of the eminent firm of Silk, Sateen, Plush, Tearit and Company, of Little Peeter Street, E.C.? Do you proffer him assiduously the comfortable solicitude and loving-kindness which a man is believed to have a right to expect from the wife of his bosom? Answer (in vinegary tones): 'Most certainly not. As for poor Charlie's important position, it has never run to more than a hundred and fifty a year, though he told me he was making three hundred before he married me. And as for solicitude and loving-kindness, and all that sort of thing—rodents! You should see poor Charlie coming home at two a.m., with poor Hubert from next door, and then talk to me of solicitude! The difference between us, foolish one! is that *I* have the honour to be poor Charlie's wife, and *you* haven't.' And here, from the beautiful feminine point of view, the discussion might well end.

On the other hand, I am one of those old-fashioned persons who believe that man at large, including even suburban man, is largely the creature of his women-folk. From his birth up, man is principally in the hands of a woman. It is she who teaches him his earliest lessons; it is she who teaches him to talk, to walk, and to behave mannerly at table; it is she who imparts to him much further instruction—namely, as to 'manliness,' as to what is and is not genteel, as to the general character of women, and as to the general scope and purport of life. You, madam, at the present moment are consciously or unconsciously engaged in doing thus much for your boys, and, with the necessary changes, for your girls; but especially do you devote yourself to the training of your boys. A boy's best friend, as all Suburbia knows, is his mother. The song says so, and nobody doubts it. I shall not deny or controvert it. At the same time, when I am compelled to come close up to male Suburbia, and observe what a pellucid, and ingenious, and immaculate, and ineffable, and dignified, and discreet, and distinguished piece of manhood it is, I am prone to wonder what it may be that you and the other ladies of its acquaintance have whispered into its long ears. I do not suppose for a moment that you require me to tell you that your whisperings have amounted to something like the following:

The Female Suburban

A man without money is like a clock without works. Money makes happiness.

Be truthful and honest, for by so doing you shall compass money.

Always marry where there is money.

Let your whole life be given over to the getting together of money.

Spend all the money you get, and put the balance in the Post-Office Savings Bank in my name.

Never stint me of money; I was not brought up to it.

When money ceases to come in at the door, love flies out of the window.

Any man can be a millionaire if he will only work hard enough. Where there's a will there's a way.

Make a point of insisting upon a rise at Christmas; we can then take a bigger house.

You labour; I admire you.

We must never forget to keep three servants and a silver table.

Eight-guinea hats are the cheapest in the long-run.

Other men treat their wives properly, so must you.

Money makes the mare go.

These selections from your book of wisdom will probably rouse you to momentary anger. For all that, I defy you to read sweeter things out of it, or things which are nearer your heart and more frequently in your thoughts. I should be sorry for you to suppose that such a system of wisdom is either wicked or scandalous. There is but one just term to apply to it, and that is—'suburban.' All the women of Suburbia—and there are monstrous regiments of them—think, madam, precisely as you think. It is eminently suburban and eminently feminine to think as the majorities think, and therefore you are not to be held blamable.

The points thus gracefully touched upon are

points which arise, I think, out of your relation to the men-folk of your family. In the main, and while you are young, they have a special application to your husband. Later in life you apply them to your sons. And this brings me to the question of your attitude to your daughters. I make no doubt that you can remember a time when the question of daughters was quite a simple one. Daughters were brought up in the household, their mothers instructed them in the domesticities and the gentilities, wept a tender tear or two when they got married, took a keen interest in possible and actual grandchildren, did their best to keep on good terms with their sons-in-law, and presumably died happy. Nowadays all that is changed, and it is the suburban female who has been the principal agent in changing it. The grand principle of female independence had its rise in Suburbia as surely as Providence made little apples.

Poor Pa could not make enough money to keep Hawthorndene going in the approved suburban style, poor Ma declined to be pinched, and screwed, and dunned, and left out of the local running in matters of dress and taste any longer. Poor Pa had nothing in the way of lands, houses, hereditaments, hard cash, plate, jewellery, or other property, to leave to the gentle Maria, the laughing-eyed Maudie, and the brave Emma Jane. Those girls should be taught to earn their own livings. Marriage is a poor look-out from downtrodden woman's point of view. Shorthand, typewriting, the instruction of the small children of the wealthy—nay, even ribbon-measuring in drapers' shops or a position in the third row of a ballet—are greatly to be preferred. Always be independent, dear girls, and then, if a man asks you to marry him, you can inquire with a good heart how much money he has got. Once again, madam, I decline to condemn your line of thought with hard or ungracious words. Once again I merely suggest to you that it is suburban. If we are to have suburbs and suburban females, it is defensible, because all the female suburbans will defend it to the last gasp and from the bottom of their souls.

I put it to you, madam, that the words I have spoken are worth consideration, and that they are words which, if you read them aright, will delight and inspire you.

And I beg to remain,

Your Obliged Servant.

CHAPTER VI

THEIR YOUNG

A BABE comes trailing clouds of glory, even though it be the fruit of a suburban marriage. Therefore, of the little pink suburbanites who keep suburban registrars so busy putting down Cecil and Howard and Bertram, and Gwendoline and Joan and Daisy, day by day, I do not propose to offer complaint. I am of opinion, however, that the young of the suburbans begin to exhibit marked suburban tendencies at a quite tender age.

If you will take me to a baby-show, where there is anything like a proper display of miscellaneous infants, I will pick out the small suburbanites—separate for you the lambs from the kids, as it were—after the most cursory inspection.

For a little suburbanite is always tetchy, overfed, stumpy about the nose, fractious, tearful, hiccoughy, flatulent, and inclined to pull ungracious mouths the minute you look at it. Having some inkling that it is being improperly nourished, that its clothes are too fine for its position, and that its parents are simply off their heads with pride in its possession, it declines to be imperturbable, and smiles only at rare intervals and after much tickling up. It may be able to say 'Goo-goo!' like other babies, but it says 'Goo-goo!' with a serious suburban accent.

I have every sympathy for the tears and protestations which will be let off by the female suburban when she peruses these lines. At the same time, the bitter truth must be told. It is a fact that in Suburbia infant loveliness and infant vigour are, by comparison, always at a low ebb. The medical profession will bear me out in this, though I do not expect the indigenous suburban will ever believe it. Proud fathers and mothers of crinkly infants invariably come out of Suburbia. Reasonable people are never proud of their offspring: it is a sure sign of a vulgar and uncultivated mind.

But, to proceed with our young. It is at the age of three that they may be said to take on the true aspects of their class. At three or thereabouts the suburban girl has frizzy, skimpy hair, and the suburban boy has flossy ringlets and a curl on top. When a wealthy and prosperous person shows you a picture of himself in a state of infancy, with a curl on top of his head and flossy ringlets over his ears, do not trust him. He comes of an old-established race of suburbanites, and there is danger ahead for you if you listen to his blandishments.

I have several particular instances in my mind when I write this, and it is therefore that I adjure you to be careful. There never was a more offensively suburban practice than this indulging of small boys in flowing curls. It can serve only one purpose—namely, the gratification of the idiot vanity of females, and it ought to be prohibited by Act of Parliament. All the men with long locks, from Absalom to Buffalo Bill, failed to come to good by them. Little boys, and particularly suburban little boys, should be well barbered from the time when they begin to walk. Suburbia, if I know it at all, will go on curling and scenting its young hopefuls' ringlets in spite of one, but that is of no consequence.

In the matter of dress for their darlings, suburban parents, or perhaps, more correctly speaking, suburban mothers, are equally at fault. Whose tiny tots are these who toddle down the terrace, garbed after the manner of Little Red Ridinghood and Claude Duval? Who are these that wear sandals, and rabbit-skin cuffs, and kilts and philibegs, and general picture costumes, in broad daylight? Has the gracious Mr. Treloar been amusing himself with another children's fancy-dress ball? Not a bit of it! These little Sirs and Madams, these Marjory Daws and Little Miss Muffets and small Jack Shepherds, and smaller Lord Charles Beresfords, are merely —or shall we say simply?—the issue in the feminine and male lines of Mr. and Mrs. Subub, of Glenesk, Sandringham Avenue, Connaught

Road, Cholmondeley Park, S.W. Heaven bless their merry little souls, for it is not yet their fault!

Later, of course, we shall find little Master Subub following in father's footsteps, to the tune of a small coat with a pointy back instead of tails, a pair of gray trousers, and a cocky little silk hat, what time Miss Sophy does her best to look like the pictures of the Honourable Ladies Blanche, Joan, and Betty Murgatroyd, which mother has shown her in the *Sketch*, the *Tatler*, the *Bystander*, the *Motorist and Traveller*, or some other suburban sixpenn'orth.

And later still I conjure you to mark young Mr. Subub. There is nobody like him, even in the fashion plates. For, behold, his coats are of the waistiest, his hats shine like the morning-star, his patent-leather boots outdazzle the morning sun, his umbrella is length without breadth, and his monocle makes him look like a bankrupt publisher; and if a little green bus ticket did not incontinently peep out of his side-pocket, he might pass for the younger son of a peer's butler.

As for Miss Subub, she has rings on her fingers and bells on her toes; bracelets and ornaments of rolled gold; a walking-skirt like a Canterbury-bell (there is nobody in all Suburbia who knows what a Canterbury-bell is), with a rustle to it; a cheap stole or a fluffy boa; weeny brown shoes with buckles to them; open-work stockings, pardie; and a plumed and flower-decked hat as big as a cab-wheel. How in the name of goodness does poor Pa do it? Echo answers 'How?' —not to say 'poor Pa.'

And when it comes to speech and manners, one is constrained to admit that the young of the suburbans are but slightly differentiated from the young of the Kickapoo tribe of Indians. Old Mr. Subub, having been kicked severely round the Metropolis for half a century or so, has achieved a certain share of the wisdom and diffidence that is to be gotten out of sorrow. Old Mrs. Subub has been nattered and bullied and disappointed into a sort of mild and pious extinction. But the fiery, untamed young Szububs—what fantastic trick is there that they cannot play grossly, flagrantly, and cacophonously before high heaven? The blood of five generations of impudent, thin-witted suburbanites courses with loose rein through their dubious veins. They have been taught to 'speak up,' and grip people hard by the hand, and 'look people straight in the face.' They have been taught to take warning by the late Mr. John Ruskin, and never say to their hearts, 'Down, little bounder, down!' They have been taught that the main chance is always and eternally the main chance, and that the world consists of two sorts of people—smart people and fools; that fine feathers make fine birds; that the art of life is keeping your neck up; and that a large acquaintance among 'classy' people is the essence of advancement.

And they are filled with a meretricious, material, unblushing, ha'penny-paper wisdom, which is calculated to appal the stoutest. They consider themselves up to every move upon the social board. To use their own cant term, they are as wide as the ocean and as deep, and afraid of nothing. And, to be quite frank, smart though they may appear, they are precisely as brainless and as unintellectual as puppies.

To have to deal with the young of Suburbia in the great world is a revelation and an education in itself. A year or two of it is apt to thrust upon one a poor opinion of humanity, and to make one wish that the suburbs had never been built. For the suburban youth of either sex is dowered with qualities which nobody but a ha'penny-newspaper proprietor or an organizer of racing competitions is in the least likely to admire.

The chief of these gifts is what may be termed 'cockiness.' Your affairs are never safe in the hands of young Suburbia, male or female. They will treat your best friend and your fattest customer with hauteur and disdain, and take your enemies to their silly bosoms, and expect you to thank them for it. They are without minds, and perpetually in a muddle; they do everything by halves, and nothing well; they are burdened with an overwhelming self-respect, which is really an excuse for shuffling out of difficult or unpleasant labour; and they are never worth more than a third of the money they have the impudence to ask for themselves.

The two curses of people who have to keep offices are stupidity and incompetence, or, in other words, blunder-making and not knowing what to do. This is largely the result of the suburban system of educating boys and girls. The education of Suburbia may be imparted chiefly at free schools, or high schools, or private academies for young ladies and gentlemen. I know not. But this I do know: that in effect it is a fancy, specious, pinchbeck, and mythical education, designed rather to flatter the vanity of fatuous parents, and to appeal to the susceptibilities of elderly aunts with money to leave, than to make a useful workaday person of the young suburban.

Vast fortunes are spent in Suburbia on the gentle arts of shorthand and typewriting. It is no exaggeration to say that in nine cases out of ten the resultant shorthand is undecipherable, and the resultant typewriting a matter of printer's pie.

Only here and there do you find a suburbanite who is efficient in these respects. And why? Because at school the dear young people were allowed to indulge themselves and their parents in smatterings of most kinds of learning, and were not grounded thoroughly even in the three R's.

Possibly it is as well; it may even amount to a dispensation of Providence. For until we have proof that a liberal education will knock the cheapness and the rapacity out of the suburban character, it is reasonable to assume that such an education would be used by young Suburbia for nefarious, snobbish, and suburban purposes. Wherefore let us not be in too great haste to improve matters.

CHAPTER VII

THEIR LOVES AND MARRIAGES

THAT love, courtship, and marriage lend some little colour and romance to the dun lives of the suburbans is not a matter for wonder. Love, courtship, and marriage have a way of doing as much for most people; and so long as the suburban retains even the guise of a human creature, he or she has a prescriptive right to a certain amount of romance. But if you were to inspect a few thousands of the engaged couples, and of the young and old married couples, now basking in the sunshine of love in various sections of the suburbs, you would be driven to remarkable conclusions.

In the first place, you would discover a very considerable amount of ill-assortment; secondly, you would discover that love and courtship are not quite the same things in Suburbia as they are outside; and, thirdly, you would be forced regretfully to note that marriage appears to be a failure more frequently in Suburbia than in any other part of the world. It is a singular but nevertheless instructive fact that we owe pretty well the whole of the morbid movements and discussions of the past half-century to the delicate genius of Suburbia. Women's rights were first broached, and bloomers first worn, in Suburbia. 'Is marriage a failure?' was an exceeding bitter cry out of the sick married soul of Suburbia. 'The marriage handicap' was a phrase invented by an ingenuous gentleman who had been observing Suburbia in the faith that he was looking into the manners and customs of the upper classes. 'Do we believe?' is another desperate inquiry out of a blank and benighted Suburbia.

Now, the suburbans have a great habit of putting up a question for the pure pleasure of being themselves allowed to answer it. Like little children who 'know a riddle,' they are for ever anxious to start interrogatories with the engaging view of getting people to 'give it up' and providing answers themselves. And, as might be expected in the circumstances, the answers are invariably quite simple. 'Do we believe?' for example, can safely be answered, from Suburbia's standpoint, with a good round 'No,' and 'Is marriage a failure?' with an equally good round and emphatic 'Yes.'

When Suburbia put those questions, it knew full well that it did not believe, and it was even surer that marriage was a failure, and a failure of the completest kind. It wanted merely to ease its tired heart by the airing of views in epistolary print, just as a poet, with something on his mind, hankers after 'the sad mechanic exercise,' or a politician, desirous of his country's good, bursts into fervid oratory. And I say and maintain that Suburbia at large is not only of the honest opinion that marriage is a failure, but it has learnt to perceive, further, that love and courtship are distinct failures also.

Let us speculate for a moment on the nature

of love as one comes across it in this golden country of Suburbia. What does it amount to? What is it worth? What are the elements of it? What is the true inwardness of it? Only too frequently it may with justice be summed up as a mere matter of a calf and a hoyden—a giggling, scant-brained boy and a calculating, pot-hearted girl. Regard these engaged couples in detail, and you will marvel in your heart how in the name of wonder they managed to run across one another. The fact, of course, is that they met by virtue of all sorts of remarkable chances.

Haply, he was strolling in the park what time the County Council band discoursed sweet music gratis. She with her dearest female friend happened also to be strolling in the park. As they passed, he and she beheld one another with meretricious glances. She blushed and giggled and nudged her friend. He, being a complete gentleman with an eighteenpenny tie on, lifted his hat and remarked sententiously, 'Good-evening.' She and her friend stopped and shook hands with great politeness. Very cheap conversation followed, an appointment was made for another meeting, and thence sprang a relation which is to persist till death do them part.

Or it is possible that they met at some half-crown dancing academy, or at an assembly-rooms ball, or on the occasion of a shop assistants' half-day trip to Brighton. Or they may have worked together in the same office, or frequented the same bun-shop, or lived in the same foolish terrace. Always the results are identical. After herculean struggles in the direction of economy, he succeeds in scraping together the price of a nine-carat engagement ring with diamonds and rubies in it, the which is presented with trembling deference to the young lady, and they become proper, irrefutable, and unchallengeable fiancées. For never by any chance does either Master or Miss Subub dare to speak of the other in any terms save that of 'fiancée.' 'My young lady,' 'my young man,' 'my intended,' and all such unsophisticated phrases, are entirely gone out where fashionable Suburbia is concerned, and it must be 'fiancée' or nothing.

One takes it for granted that out of the years of courtship in which these tender couples seem fated to indulge they derive a due moiety of comfort and joy. On the whole, however, a suburban courtship is not by any means a dream of bliss; neither is it roses all the way, nor wholly lavender. Rather, in the gross, one finds that it is an exceedingly nervous and trying business, abounding in tiffs and small differences, marred and vulgarized by petty jealousies, punctuated by out-and-out quarrels, and oftentimes rendered bitter and unsatisfactory by a persistent lack of means and hope.

Furthermore, the action of courting suburbanites towards the several objects of their affections is singularly unconventional—at any rate, in essence. You will hear smart young Master Subub talk sweetly of Gertie as his 'best girl,' thereby being desirous of indicating that 'there are others.' Gertie, on the other hand, is by no means sure that she will eventually enter into the bonds of matrimony with Cecil, despite the fact that their engagement has already been of three or four years' duration. The truth is that neither of them is really satisfied. Cecil, for his part, could wish that Gertie were a little less mercenary and exacting and imperative and heartless than she makes herself out to be. Gertie, on her part, considers that Cecil is none too bright in the intellect, has a nasty way of boring and hipping her, and lacks those qualities of energy, application, and pushfulness which are likely to make for success in life. She has no particular fancy for the position of poor man's wife. She has seen enough of poverty and hardupness and meagreness in her father's household, and if 'Mr. Right' came along with a lot of money or enticing prospects, she has a pretty shrewd suspicion that the line she would take might induce in Cecil's breast feelings of marked annoyance.

Cecil, on the other hand, has been known to throw over Gertie on the smallest provocation in the way of a widow with a houseful of furniture, or an orphan maiden whose suburban papa has left her £75 a year free of income-tax.

This last contingency, of course, leads us, more often than not, slap-bang into the Sheriff's court, where there is a hilarious action for breach of promise, and our poor faded love-letters, with the bits of futile poetry in them, are read out by raspy-voiced counsel for the edification of a guffawing court. It is as sad as sad can be, but it is truly suburban.

As for suburban weddings, with their apings of affluence, their hired coaches and organ-playings and bell-ringings, their bouquets, their red baize, their infant train-bearers, their slate-coloured trousers, their rice and confetti throwing, their guzzlings, their bad-cigar smokings and silly speech-making, and their goings-away to Bexhill on a cash balance of £10—the less said of them the better. They are *de rigueur* in Suburbia, inasmuch as the 'quiet wedding' is unknown there, and the registry-office wedding not believed by the female population to be quite so legal as it might be. But they suit Suburbia, even though they cost twice or three times as much as they need cost; and woe be unto the bridegroom or bride's parent who is not prepared to stand the racket.

After the honeymoon, which we will assume is a radiant and celestial business, the suburban couple begin, in vulgar parlance, to 'settle down,' the which process is usually a slow, tedious, and uninspiring one. As a rule it means at least eighteen months of domestic jarring, wrangling, and argument. In time some semblance of a *modus vivendi* is hit upon, and henceforward we go more or less sourly on our dreary way in an association which resembles more nearly the association of lodger and landlady, or of galley-slave and over-woman, than of husband and wife in the proper sense of things.

For in nine cases out of ten your suburban woman is an utter shrew, termagant, and scold. She 'begins as she means to go on,' on the advice of the fat and puffy matrons who invariably gather round her in her early wifehood, and she goes on with something of a vengeance all the rest of her life. The married life of the suburb may appear to be tranquil and peaceful and undisturbed; really it is nothing of the kind. An armed neutrality, a cold resignation, is the best that can be said for it. Its essential quality is its respectability, and this, as a rule, is maintained unimpaired to the end of the chapter. For in Suburbia we must, above all things, be consistently and undeviatingly and abidingly respectable.

CHAPTER VIII

THE GREAT HEART OF CLAPHAM

The person who first credited Clapham with an abounding heart did so, as who should say, sarcastically and with his tongue in his cheek. It was a trifle of phrase-making which meant very little, but nevertheless hit a certain mark, and has consequently seen considerable service. Every now and again the hard-pushed journalist trots it out in a leader or paragraph, still writing it down sarcastically and with his tongue in his cheek. And he blesses the inventor, if it be only subconsciously.

The great heart of Clapham, however, is in deed and truth, not a sarcastic fiction, but a real thing. It exists and pulses and abounds like any other great heart, and they that write wickedly and contemptuously about it know not what they do. After much reflection and some comparison, I find myself disposed to the opinion that it is fair and reasonable to call Clapham the capital of Suburbia. First, it is a large suburb; secondly, everybody has heard of it; thirdly, it is an ancient and fishlike suburb; fourthly, it boasts a gay parterre or Common and a mammoth and 'important' railway-junction; and, fifthly, it is in effect about the only suburb that can be accused of possessing an obvious, gigantic, and palpitating heart.

Suburbanism of every kind and every degree, no matter how gross or how whirling, is more than plentiful in Clapham. Just as the great world gathers together and concentrates and finds its most catholic expression in London, so does the great world of suburbanism come to its fullest and most vivid realization in Clapham.

If you walk down the Clapham Road, from the end of the Common to Clapham Road Station, with your eyes open, you will have seen the best part of all that Suburbia has to show you.

You will understand, as it were, intuitively and without further ado, the cheapness and out-of-jointness of the times; you will comprehend the why and wherefore and *raison d'être* of halfpenny journalism. The true inwardness of four-threeness will be revealed to you like a flash. And you will perceive that whizzers, penny buses, gramophones, bamboo furniture, pleasant Sunday afternoons, Glory Songs, modern language teas, golf, tennis, high school education, dubious fiction, shilling's-worths of comic writing, picture postcards, miraculous hair-restorers, prize competitions, and all other sorts of twentieth-century clap-trap, have got a market and a use, and black masses of supporters.

This is the intention and lesson of Clapham—that man was born a little lower than the angels, and has been descending into suburbanism ever since. He has a heart left, and attenuated and vulgarized emotions. Here you may see both his heart and his emotions in full and unconquerable blast, and you no longer wonder that calculating persons have perceived that there is money in them, and proceeded with their fortune-making accordingly. There is many an affluent author, many a windy pulpiteer, many a 'smart' humorist, many an 'eminent' actor, many a proud newspaper proprietor, many an unctuous publicist, many a beauty, many a sage, and many a saint, who would be nothing and less than nothing if it were not because of the spirit which pervades every nook and corner of this same gray, grinning, unlovely Clapham.

Perhaps the air has something to do with it, perhaps it is the Common, perhaps it is the mammoth railway-junction. But in any case you shall find in Clapham the very essences of shallowness, and cheapness, and mediocrity, and dulness, and stupidity, and snobbishness, which make suburbanism, and which therefore render possible the amazing careers of the rhetoricians, and poseurs, and false prophets, and incompetencies, and ha'penny-snatchers of our own amazing generation.

This great drear, unspiritual, unimaginative, deep-rooted Clapham, in fact, is a standing witness and example of what mankind would become if you left it to its own sweet will and devices. By the very force of its geographical position, of the general impecuniosity of its residents, and the unadulterated suburban spirit which breathes through and inspires its daily comings and goings, Clapham has been left free to work out its own damnation unreproved by the moralists, undisturbed by the reformers, and unillumined by the seers and the poets. From its youth up it has enjoyed a reputation for respectability, and no man has dared to hold it up to opprobrium. Cunning persons, however, have latterly and of their cunning hazarded correct surmises as to the true meanings of it. They have said to themselves, 'Behold, herein is the strong city of the foolish and the vapid and the empty-headed. The citizens thereof have a little money and a paucity of brains, and, if we mistake not, they will e'en purchase such and such mediocre merchandise. Lo, we lay that merchandise at the simple feet of Clapham.'

They have done it, and their reward proves that

they were as worldly-wise as they were wicked and unscrupulous. In addition, they have concluded with a creditable sagacity that what Clapham accepts to-day will be accepted by all Suburbia and all Provincia to-morrow, and that if you can sell your pills, or your comic cuts, or your brief, bright, and brotherly theology, or your mercerated-cotton pocket-handkerchiefs, or your catch-penny writing and acting, in Clapham, you can sell them wherever a proper handful of foolish, human, unthinking persons are congregated together.

A man with any sort of a scheme that is calculated to enrich himself at the expense of the public morality or the public brain may with safety and economy try his scheme first on Clapham. If it meet with approval in those egregious shades—and it certainly will meet with approval if it be pretentious and vulgar enough—there is certain money in it. If, on the other hand, it fail to meet with the approval of Clapham, it will fail to meet with the approval of snobbery, brainlessness, and suburbanism in the mass. Whether you have on offer a hat varnish, a new idiot game of cards, a new line in unsavoury fiction, unwholesome belles-lettres, or impertinent journalism, try it first, make your initial experiment, put out your feelers, fly your kite, take your consensus of opinion, in Clapham.

It is impossible that you should be put on any but the sound tack by so doing; for in this, the chief stronghold of suburbanism, you have the natural, civilized, untrammelled, respectable, original sin, run to seed, as it were, and ripe for your harvest. The Pentecostal Dervishes put their trust in Lambeth; the Torrey-Alexander combination pitched its tents at the Albert Hall; Mr. W. T. Stead's *Daily Paper* went for Hampstead and the Crystal Palace and Flatland; Sir Alfred Harmsworth's *Daily Mirror* set its cap at Mayfair and the stately homes of England; Mr. Chamberlain protectionizes in Birmingham, Glasgow, and Liverpool; Mr. Justice Darling breaks the alabaster box of his wit in the courts of King's Bench or at the Old Bailey three hundred and thirty-one times in a single day. But you may take it from me that the authentic, apposite, and really prolific ground for such movements and persons is Clapham. Begin in Clapham, establish yourself properly in the Clapham mind and heart, and you have conquered and compassed and roped in at least nine-tenths of the rest of the world to boot. In her way, this suburb of the suburbs is as regal and as imperial as Rome herself, though she be set round a muddy Common rather than on seven eternal hills. She has had more to do with the history of this world than Mecca, or Boston, or Fleet Street, or St. Stephen's, or Printing House Square, or even Dumfries or Kerrimuir. She is the respectable, stupid, skimpy-souled Suburbia incarnate, and mighty and fearsome shall be her name at the ultimate summing.

CHAPTER IX

TOOTING THE BLEST

EVERYTHING seems to point to the absolute and irrefragable bliss of Tooting. Separated from Clapham, that hub of Suburbia, by a salubrious and engaging district called Balham, it is nevertheless connected with the great-hearted mother-suburb by whizzer. You can live at Tooting in the open wilds, as it were, and among the sweet, new red-brick houses, and still be within three minutes of the gray, confirmed suburban amenities of Clapham.

And what dulcet and sylvan and secluded murmur is to be got out of the very word 'Tooting' by him whose ear is attuned to the more delicate sensibilities of suburbanism. Tooting! It is as though the mellifluous should babble to one of tussocked meads, and April lambkins, and piping shepherds, and snug homesteads, and cream and honey, and custards, and boiled beef and suet dumplings. Tooting! A land, you feel sure, flowing with beer and skittles, and full of placid, comfortable, mouth-wiping persons who have retired from the fret and fever of the world with a reasonable competence, and are husbanding out life's taper to the close in the most leisurely, pleasant, and reposeful fashion.

Tooting! What could be sweeter on the lips, or more elegant on the antique vellum whereon we indite our little notes and billets-doux? Tooting! where we have bought a house on the 'Why pay rent?' system, and whither we have migrated, with our suburbanism still heavy upon us, out of respect to the dictates of more money and less worry. Tooting! the rustic, the admirable, the primal, the innocent, the sportive, the select, the reposeful, the blest! See Naples and die! See Tooting and live!

And yet, withal, if we are to look upon Tooting

as the latest expression of the high spirits of suburbanism—and I think we are justified in so doing—what do we find? Well, we find that, taking one thing with another, the latest expression of the high spirits of suburbanism is even more pitiful and heart-breaking than the earlier ones were. Clapham may be the devil, but Tooting is his prodigal, ne'er-do-well child. It is a whirling wilderness of villadom, a riot of inexpensive red brick, set down with attempts after reasonableness and artistic effect of the most ill-judged kind. The man or woman who can be happy in Tooting could be happy anywhere, like the common goat.

On the face of it, such persons are entirely without that sixth sense which directs one to appropriateness. It seems to me impossible that a sentient being should pay two hundred and fifty a year or so for the privilege of occupying a house which rejoices in the name of 'The Diggings,' or 'The Den,' or 'The Slopstone.'

I do not suppose for a moment that such establishments exist, even in the most lunatic parts of Suburbia. But it may be presumed that, if they did exist, nobody would take them at the rent. Yet God's creatures — soaring human beings, persons of means and shrewdness and perspicacity—go to live in Tooting by the myriad. It does not appear to occur to them that the address is fatal—that even Hanwell is a less dangerous dating-place, and lays one open to less sarcasm and less rallying.

Tooting! Methinks the poetaster who took up his abode at Tennyson House, Shakespeare Road, Milton Park, must have had the hide and the imperturbability of the elephant; but the man that puts 'Tooting' on his notepaper must be a man of blood and iron and thrice-chilled steel. T-double o-t, Toot; i-n-g, ing—Tooting! Spell it over. Say it to yourself many times, look at it right way up and upside down, and be amazed!

Was ever such a piece of rank and flagrant suburbanism perpetrated by an unconsidering, inimical, contemptuous inventor of place-names? Really, it is without parallel in the whole history of nomenclature. Pudsey and Chowbent, Mumps, Chobham, Sudbury, and Cleethorpes pale their ineffectual and ignominious fires in front of it.

Tooting! Tooting! Tooting! Tooting! One can imagine innumerable village idiots murmuring it sweetly to themselves as they mumble their poor unhandy fingers. Tooting! Tooting! Tooting! Tooting! Tooting! If Shakespeare had known about it—which he probably did or didn't, as the case may be—he would most assuredly have been fired by it into an ecstasy of comedy and comfortable farce.

Snug, a joiner; Quince, a carpenter; Snout, a tinker; Starveling, a tailor; Bottom, a weaver; Flute, a bellows-mender—I will never believe, though you stone me to death for my heresy, that they were citizens of Athens. Shakespeare got them out of some Elizabethan Tooting; for what doth the flute but Toot, and where should tailoring, and tinkering, and joinering, and carpentering, and bellows-mending flourish if not in this blessed and blissful Tooting?

Furthermore, I am disposed to imagine that in some of my wanderings under the stars up the Tooting Grand Parade I have had glimpses of Peaseblossom, Cobweb, Moth, and Mustardseed —fairies all, newly come from their revels in the local meadows; and I am quite sure that every woman of Tooting who is in love with a Tooting man loves something in the nature of that which Titania loved.

All the same, I bear Tooting no malice. For aught I know to the contrary, its morals, manners, and intellect are as sound and wholesome as those of any other suburb in the King's dominions. I have no greater fault to find with its material parts, its location, its conveniences, its architecture, its disposition, its temperament, its drainage, its landlords, and the people that dwell under them, than I have fault to find with similar things in Torquay, or Port Said, or Zanzibar. It is the name that tickles me, and I cannot help it.

If anybody gave me a house and lands at Tooting with a nine hundred and ninety-nine years' lease, and rates and taxes remitted, I would proceed thither in pantechnicons, and set up thither my everlasting rest without the smallest compunction or hesitancy. But methinks that for my consequent ease and health and comfort I should still have to make sacrifices, and that some Christian soul calling on me o' nights might find me in 'another part of the wood' crying foolishly: 'Scratch my head, Peaseblossom Give me your neaf, Mounsieur Mustardseed. . . . I have a reasonable good ear in music. Let's have the tongs and the bones. . . . I could munch your good dry oats. I have a great desire to a bottle of hay. Good hay, sweet hay, hath no fellow. . . . But, I pray you, let none of your people stir me. I have an exposition of sleep come upon me.' And surely I should fall into a wonderful beauty-sleep, and murmur only therein, 'Tooting! Tooting! Tooting! Tooting!'

CHAPTER X

KILBURN THE GOLDEN

In a tender small poem called 'The Hebrew's Saturday Night'—a sort of metrical *jeu d'esprit*, so to speak—Mr. Israel Zangwill makes a human person thank God he is a Jew. This is as it should be. A man should always thank God for being whatever he chances to be that he could not himself help.

Mr. Zangwill resides, or did until lately reside, in Kilburn, and so do many other Jews. Formerly, though I am not of the tribe of Manasseh, I lived there myself, and I have never been sorry for it. I have ventured to call it Kilburn the Golden, not because of this latter fact, nor even because one John Keats was wont to 'wander in the Kilburn meadows,' but simply because Kilburn, as I understand it, is the favourite residential suburb of the London Jews.

As a body, the London, or we may say Kilburn, Jews appeal to me as being pretty well everything that is admirable. They are the only class of suburbans on this planet of marvels and surprises who have the art to live well within their incomes, and here surely I lay at their travelled and shining feet the highest of praise. A man who lives within his income is the master of this world, and is bound to receive consideration in the next.

The Jews are a chosen and segregated people, the fine flower, the golden fruit, the coreless apple, of the nations. They are English without the English lavishness; they are Scotch without the Scotch whisky; and Irish without the Irish misfortunateness. They are French, too, without the French volatility, German without the German pigheadedness, Russian without the Russian unwieldiness, and Turks and Greeks with none of the little weaknesses which keep Turks and Greeks under. This is why they make money and stick to it, and this is why Kilburn may be called the Golden.

A medical gentleman practising in this auriferous region swears to me that from a Jew customer he received the following treatment:

Imprimis, he was called at two o'clock in the morning to visit a sick Hebrew patriarch. Gasping on his bed, the Hebrew made immediate inquiry:

'Doctor, I take it that you do not charge extra for being called out of bed? And, by-the-by, doctor, I hope you incline to the good old custom of no fees whatever as between professional men; for I myself am a distinguished member of the literary profession, and once wrote a novel which went through three editions.'

The doctor smiled, said 'Yes, yes,' looked meticulously into his patient's condition, decided that there was nothing much the matter with him, told him so, but suggested that for the alleviation of certain small symptoms medicine might be provided at eight o'clock if somebody would call for it.

At eight-thirty a rosy, sixteen-stone, sloe-eyed youth, son of the patriarch, called. He had come for father's medicine, and would the doctor please make sure to visit dear father again in the course of the morning, as he was feeling very bad? And, by-the-by—for some reason or other 'by-the-by' has come to be a great Hebrew expression—could the doctor inform him what was good for an ingrowing toe-nail, and whether 'Grape Nuts' was a really desirable breakfast dish, and whether he (the doctor) would have any objection to the fat young Jew's use of his (the doctor's) name in applying for samples of certain medicated wines? In fact, he (the young Jew) was so sure that the doctor would oblige him in this matter that he had already on the road up from the patriarch's house dropped into a pillar-box a postcard signed in the doctor's name, requesting that two sample bottles of the said medicated wine should be sent forthwith to the doctor's address.

'Of course,' added young Melchisedek, 'you will remember that, if they come, they are my property.'

The doctor, good easy man, smiled and smiled, and said 'Yes, yes,' and put up his nux vomica in a phial and his sugar-coated pills in a pretty pink box, as patient as you please.

'Tell your father to shake the bottle,' he said, 'and let him take two pills at once. Certainly I will call again in the course of the morning, though you may take it from me that his condition is not alarming.'

At eleven o'clock the good man stood once more at the sick patriarch's bedside. He felt his pulse by request, looked at his tongue by request, and listened charitably to a history of minor and unimportant ailments personal to the patriarch, and extending over a period of half a century. And the patriarch concluded by expressing his entire approbation of the altruistic spirit which prompted one professional man to visit and succour another without fee or reward.

Whereupon the doctor stole softly downstairs. On the first landing he was confronted by the patriarch's buxom daughter. This young lady deposed that she had a frightful palpitation of the heart; that she sometimes fancied that she must have cancer; that she suffered from headaches and nerves; and did the doctor think that a bottle of medicine would be amiss?

The doctor promised that he would send her a drop of something right off, and proceeded to descend the stairs. In the hall, like Napoleon at St. Helena, stood the patriarch's wife. She explained with a good Yiddish intonation that she had been a great sufferer. She might remark to the doctor—he, of course, being a family man (he is absolutely without chick or child)—that her chiefest troubles were wind and water. Could he not out of the professional courtesy one professional man owed to another send her a bottle of medicine? And, by-the-by, the maid, poor thing! is entirely out of sorts—the lower classes always are. She is an old servant, and she is subject to hysterics and a ravening appetite. Couldn't the doctor send something to cure the appetite, even if it only ameliorated the hysterics?

Selah! This is Kilburn the Golden all over. It will interest the reader to know that the sundry bottles of medicine were delivered; that the patriarch recovered and got about again; that the two bottles of medicated wine arrived duly, and were despatched to their rightful owner; and that the doctor received for his pains the appended testimonial:

'Dear Dr. ——,

'As you agreed not to very kindly [*sic*] charge me for your recent professional attendance upon myself and family, I feel that I cannot do less than say to you how thankful I am to God for our complete recovery. If at any time I can recommend you to my friends, it will give me pleasure.

'Yours faithfully,

'—— ——.

Thus do we manage to live within our incomes, and to do it with a good face. If an ordinary man played such pranks, one trembles to think what might become of him. But from a Kilburn suburbanite you expect nothing else, and you get nothing else, and smile accordingly.

I do not suggest for a moment that the Hebrew patriarch of our story was not prepared and in a position to pay his doctor's bill, or that it was his fault that he did not pay it. What I do suggest is that the Kilburn suburbanite is always prepared to pay for everything when the worst comes to the worst, but not before. The doctor in question, had he been firm enough, could have got his fees with greater promptitude, and certainly with greater ease, from the patriarch than he could have got them out of the average lavish non-suburban family. The average lavish non-suburban family would never have dreamed of setting up professionalism in liquidation of fees. Neither would they have gone in for medical advice all round to be comprehended under two gratuitous visits. Neither would they have ordered sample bottles of medicated wine in the name of their doctor. All the same, they would not have scrupled to keep him waiting an indefinite time for his money, which possibly amounts to the same thing. So that Kilburn the Golden need not hang its curly head.

I believe that the inhabitants of Kilburn and Maida Vale, Hebrew though the majority of them may be, still represent the very finest class of suburbanites. They have money in the banks and in all sorts of other places; they buy everything for cash, and sell everything on the hire system; they are as shrewd and as even-tempered as they are adipose; their vulgarity and swagger are based on a great deal more than nothing; their suburbanism is solid and sound and legitimate; and they are an easy-hearted, butter-fed, properly-financed, and unashamed people. On the whole, they have good reason to thank God both for their Jewry and their golden suburb.

CHAPTER XI

'APPY 'AMPSTEAD

THE 'appiness of 'Ampstead might at first blush appear to be a doubtful quantity. Indeed, I should imagine that, if Hampstead itself were canvassed on the subject, it would be found to incline to the opinion that it is not happy at all. 'Appy 'Ampstead, in so far as it exists, may be reckoned quite an alien and intermittent affair. For it is only when the East End invades Hampstead on high-days and holidays that happiness is really and truly Hampstead's portion.

Considered generally, and as it is, Hampstead owes itself almost entirely to its Heath, just as Clapham owes itself almost wholly to its Common. It is on the Heath that the Hampstead of the old time has subsisted, and it is round the Heath that the Hampstead of the new time has been built and developed.

The Hampstead of the old time is rather a matter of Good Fridays and Whit Mondays and Bank Holidays; of 'Arries and Lizas; of merry-go-rounds and swing-boats and cocoanut-shies; of shandy-gaff and beer with gin in it, and seedy cake and 'am sandwiches; of concertina-playing, and high-kicking, and hat-swopping between the sexes; of fat-women shows and pugilistic exhibitions; and of goings home in the gloaming in long wagonettes with cornet-players to them.

The Hampstead of the new time, on the other hand, is both permanent and respectable. It is always there, and it is always Hampstead. Villadom and culture and plaited hair flourish here. It is an ideal spot in which to establish fancy-goods and circulating-library businesses, baby-linen shops, superior pharmacies, high-class dairies, Italian warehouses, hair-dressing and manicure shops, and academies for instruction on the fiddle, in cookery, and in modern languages. Congregationalism and Unitarianism are also afforded special opportunities for unfoldment here.

In other words, Hampstead is nothing if not a little tony and a trifle gilt-edged. It is a suburb of the suburbs, and although it may not be the metropolis of the suburbs—because Clapham is ineradicably founded in that great position—it is still brilliant and glorious, standing in about the same relation to Clapham as Bath and Cheltenham stand to London.

Hampstead is a suburb set upon a hill, and very pleasantly set at that. Over above its gates you shall read, 'Please refrain from entering unless you are possessed of some taste and at least five hundred a year.' You may be a stockbroker, or a lawyer, or an editor, or a dentist, or something in Mincing Lane, or a minister of religion, or a retired blacking manufacturer, but we shall insist upon your being in receipt of a decent income, and upon your possession of sufficient taste to know the difference between Shakespeare and the musical glasses.

We shall also depend upon you to look with

horror and disgust upon the blaring orgies in which the low and soulless denizens of Whitechapel indulge on our Heath from time to time. We shall expect you to keep yourself and your children entirely unspotted from the said orgies, and, if needs be, to subscribe to all the sundry expressions of local disapproval thereof. And when you have settled among us, you must make a point of going about in the faith that Hampstead is not so much happy as genteel and select. All the men who have the honour to live in Hampstead are gentlemen, and all the women ladies. All the little children are 'tiny tots,' with license to call their fathers 'Dad' and their mothers 'Mummy dear!'

But the Hampstead gentlemen are gentlemen; the Hampstead ladies are ladies. This is proved by the rents they pay, and their haughty looks, and the books they read, and the swagger shops they patronize, and the superior daily and weekly papers they 'take in.' The Hampstead tiny tots are small geniuses to a tiny tot. Here one may proffer some of their quaint sayings culled from that well-known literary journal *The Academy*, which is published 'at the offices of *Country Life*.'

Wynken and Blynken, it should be observed to begin with, 'are a girl and boy, and Nod is a younger boy.' Of curling up in bed Wynken remarks: 'I don't like being straight out! I lie like the moon—like D—when I lie in bed.' How charming! how sagacious! how winning! and what admirable Hampstead! Or again, 'We don't mind—we were as cheerful as rats in a kitchen, but Nannie had on rather her look-up scowl.'

'A lady of great finish in social manner called on Wynken's mother when she was out.

'"Did you like her?"

'"Yes, I did. But, you know, she was rather an Oh-how-sweet, Oh-how-precious kind of lady. I don't *care* much, you know, for those sort of kiss-about-women. Do you?"

'It was he, too, who showed his mother the eulogy of a lover when she seasoned some rebuke with praise.

'"I have to say this to make it clear to you, just because you are all the world to me."

'"And you"—with both arms tightly encompassing—"and you are Heaven and the North Pole to *me*."

'Nod is less articulate, and altogether of a more sober caste of mind. He is five years old, and misplaces words perfectly now and then. A hair-cutter, pleased with the silky mousiness of his head, said "What nice hair!" in his foreign voice. Nod drove home a little later with slightly colouring cheeks.

'"I heard that man telling you what gentle hair I had."

'Their mother has learnt many things in their company, but one fact definitely is hers: it is, that on the whole her children teach her more than she teaches them. What a flood of light Blynken's answer let in on the subject of merit and reward! For if we are honest because honesty is the best policy, how shall honesty profit, then, the soul? Something disagreeable was required of him, and to gain his own ends he carried on a conversation from the floor, on the flat of his back.

'"Are you going to put your boots on?"

'"No."

'"You'd be sorry if the others went without you."

'"No."

'"Well, get ready quickly, and you shall each have a banana to eat upon the way."

'And a voice from the floor, with no hint of movement in it:

'"This enticing makes no difference."'

Wynken, Blynken, and Nod, I make no doubt, will come to a good and pious literary end; for there is Hampstead clearly in the blood, bones, and marrow of them. And as for their mammas and papas, I pray you of your charity to consider the following out of the Hampstead paper:

'The Mayor and Mayoress of Hampstead held a reception at the Town Hall on Wednesday evening last, at which a large and representative company was present. The entrance to the large hall was most elaborately decorated, and a magnificent supply of flowers was utilized in the most effective and artistic manner possible. The staircase was lined with growing plants, and the mirror at the head was encircled with pink azaleas, spiræas, arum lilies, daffodils, palms, etc., and with smilax, which fell in graceful trails from underneath the clock. . . . The platform was also outlined with azaleas, spiræas, and other plants, finished off with palms, and banks of palms filled the corners of the hall and made a handsome centre-piece. These ornamented the spacious drawing-room into which the hall had been converted, by means of rugs, settees, easy-chairs, etc., for the occasion.

'The Mayor and Mayoress received their guests at the principal entrance, as they were announced by the sergeant. The Mayor wore his robes and chain of office, and the Mayoress was attired in an elegant gown of soft white satin trimmed with crêpe de chine, and she carried a bouquet of pink tulips, lilies of the valley, and asparagus fern, tied with white ribbon. Later in the evening the Mayor removed his robes, and wore his chain and badge over ordinary evening dress.

'The music was arranged by Mr. Henry Holyoake, and was of a very enjoyable character. Mr. Barre Squire's trio, consisting of himself (violin), Mr. K. Park ('cello), and Mr. F. Rochester (piano), played a selection of music during the evening, which, even in the midst of animated conversation, compelled attention. . . . Miss Stanley Lucas sang "My Dearest Heart" and "Love's Echo" in perfect style and delightful voice, and Mr. Frederick Ranalow's rendering of "I know of Two Bright Eyes" and "The Little Irish Girl," and later of "Worship" and "Pretty Little Kate," was very acceptable, and displayed to great advantage his tuneful and attractive voice. Mr. H. Byron's solos on the cornet were very fine, and a musical sketch and a humorous song by Mr. Quenton Aslyn completed the music contributions. Light refreshments were served in the small hall throughout the evening, and a recherché menu was provided.'

Then follows a list of 'those who accepted the invitations of the Mayor and Mayoress,' prefaced by the remark that 'in most cases each gentleman was accompanied by a lady.' Further, we learn that 'the Mayoress was At Home on Monday and Tuesday afternoons at her residence.'

I take it for granted that Happy Hampstead has read the foregoing, and will read it again without a chuckle. If she had humour at all, she would weep salt tears of joy over it. But she is just plain, genteel, select, happy Hampstead; therefore, perhaps, she may be excused if she declines to smile.

CHAPTER XII

NAUGHTY ST. JOHN'S WOOD

St. John's Wood is singular because of a more or less fortunate propinquity to Lord's Cricket-Ground, the Zoological Society's Gardens, Primrose Hill, and that admirable public-house, the Swiss Cottage. Numerous artists of repute, including Sir Alma Tadema and Mr. Solomon J. Solomon, reside within its bosky fastnesses, as do also Mr. Clement Shorter and a lady who is commonly credited with having written a fifty-thousand-word novel and given birth to twins in one week. And in the midst of the place, like a cynosure, stands the Eyre Arms, with assembly-rooms at the back of it, where on occasion are proffered readings from Tennyson, ballad concerts, and sale by auction.

Altogether it is a delightful region, full of pretty old-fashioned houses, the majority of them with a northern light; well-established, umbrageous gardens; convenient cab-ranks, blocks of new red-brick flats, and handsome shops. Here of a spring morning you may see the crocus peep, and hear the thrush sing his song twice over, as though no such Cimmerian junction as Baker Street existed; and here, too, truth to tell, dwells the rank, fashion, genius, and beauty of Suburbia.

I have called St. John's Wood 'naughty' in deference to a highly popular prejudice. It is the fool, however, who has a poor opinion of St. John's Wood; for in point of fact it is not naughty at all, but eminently respectable, proper, discreet, and creditable. I know of no suburb of London which is more deserving of pæans and glowing tributes from a poet or prose-man with a soul in his skin, than St. John's Wood. A delicate little vellum-bound volume, in the manner of the meditative ruralists, might profitably be written about it.

It lunches at half-past one and dines at half-past seven, like a Christian, faithful district; it buys and devours cheap reprints, and it purchases and warbles cheap music; it revels in Shelley and wallows in Wagner; it never goes out without its gloves; it has conservatories at the back of its houses, banks of geraniums along its garden walls, and sprinklers on its ample lawns. The electric light is not wanting here, being, in fact, used lavishly and without regard to expense by all who have it laid on, and the front-doors are each garnished with two bells, one marked 'Visitors,' and the other marked 'Tradesmen.' I have often wondered which bell the King's taxes pulls when he makes his punctual if lugubrious calls, but that, clearly, is no affair of mine.

The people who live in St. John's Wood should on the whole, therefore, consider themselves extremely fortunate. Next to the Kilburn people, they are undoubtedly the most substantial and sweet-blooded of suburbans, and they have the additional advantages of being cultured and mainly gentile. I should consider that as a health resort St. John's Wood is almost without rival in the kingdom. The death-rate is very low, and there is no active cemetery nearer than Willesden. There is a barracks somewhat adjacent, it is true, but for reasons that are inexplicable you never clap eyes on a soldier, excepting of Sundays, when a few files are marched out to church.

And I am sincerely of opinion that St. John's Wood contains some of the nicest, prettiest and cosiest confectioners' shops in Great Britain. Here you may purchase chocolates of every known species, together with calves'-foot jelly, sponge-cake, pound-cakes, birthday-cakes with little boys and girls' names on them, wholemeal bread, and Abernethy biscuits. Here, too, you may partake of afternoon tea, served in eggshell china and on dainty if somewhat cocklety tables, for the small sum of one shilling; and if you be so minded, I believe you may, at a pinch, hire from the obliging shopman all that is requisite in the way of extra plate, glass, china, and general table requisites, for the furnishing forth of your little luncheons, dinners, ball-suppers, and other refections.

If we leave out the items indicated, St. John's Wood is to every intent and purpose a good deal of a colourless suburb. There is nothing in it that can be considered violent or outré, or even distinctive. It is simply bland, placid, unruffled, amiable, unobtrusive St. John's Wood, and there is an end of it. Its naughtiness, as I have already hinted, may be set down for a pure, unadulterated myth.

The nearest approach to anything of the kind, perhaps, is the local studios; but these, heaven knows, though they may be, and no doubt are, the perennial abiding-places of the comic spirit, have absolutely nothing about them to shock the sensibilities of the most susceptible. They consist principally of half-finished, epoch-making canvases, joke-loving persons in shabby short coats, tea and cake, pipes of tobacco, perfectly discreet models, and here and there a brandy-and-soda. Of the studios of Kensington, excepting that some of them seem to be damp coach-houses done up with washed-out art hangings and unsalable pictures, I have no knowledge, having had little time lately to visit them.

But for the studios of St. John's Wood I can

vouch, and there is not only a lot of respectability, but a considerable deal of recognised and unrecognised talent in them. For the rest of the place I have no complaint to make, other than may be extracted from the fact that it is indubitably suburban, and that it houses a mighty if fairly cultivated host of suburban souls. The one puzzle about it is that it contains at the present moment probably a greater number of unoccupied houses than any other suburb round London.

The reason for this, I am told, is that the comfortably placed, five hundred to a thousand a year, up-to-date, intellectual, in-the-swim suburban has of late taken it into his dunder head that great joy is to be derived from the pitching of one's domestic tent in a flat. Five rooms up a giddy lift and near the stars, with electric lights let into the ceiling, electric bells throughout, hot and cold water night and day, private restaurant, a gold-laced porter, and no taxes, are luring the sharp-sighted suburban out of his old villas and secluded gardens, which therefore fall into emptiness and desolation, not by ones and twos, but by dozens every quarter-day.

'It comes much cheaper,' says good man Subub. 'Mrs. Subub likes it, because it is the thing, don't you know; and, besides, there can be no getting away from the fact that the flat is the proper dwelling-place of a highly complex civilization such as ours.' I am afraid that Subub will never find out his mistake, because the whole essence of suburbanism is to keep on making mistakes, and never by any chance to find them out. All the same, I think it is a thousand pities, and not in the least a good augury for the future, inasmuch as, if the better part of Suburbia does ultimately betake itself wholly to flats, the standard of living among the suburbans is bound to become more flashy, more snobbish, more suburban, and less dignified than ever.

Indeed, no man of feeling can pace the pleasant back-streets of St. John's Wood in this latter day without indulging something in the nature of thoughts which do lie too deep for tears. The camps and strongholds of suburban domesticity are being slowly but surely invaded and broken up. The busy housewife and her handmaidens no longer ply their evening care in the roasting basement kitchens; no longer do generous sea-coal fires and cosy lamps glow in the red-curtained dining-rooms; the gold and white drawing-rooms are empty alike of gilt chairs, sylphlike forms in muslin, and grand pianos; rats and mice, if there be any, squeak and scratch in the upper stories, and the once laughterful nursery garrets are as blank and empty and sad as last year's nests.

And all for what? Why, for a steel-framed flat, with dancing people overhead, piano-playing people north and south, and screaming, scramble-abouty people beneath; for a poky kitchen with a gas-stove, a dining-room that comes somewhat hard on the elbows, a drawing-room that overlooks a fine, belching forest of chimneys, and bedrooms that you dare not snore in because of the reverberation.

Is it not a scandal that, before the small child of Suburbia, returning prettily from school, can climb the parental knee the envied kiss to share, he should be compelled to solicit the ofttimes grudging services of a lift-man? Give me, O you who preside over the lives and loves and destinies of Suburbia—give me, I beg of you, my St. John's Wood on the ground-floor!

CHAPTER XIII

NONCONFORMITY

TELL us, where is fancy bred? From whence rise up like deadly upas-trees the sects—the Methodists, the Baptists, the Wesleyans, the Congregationalists, the Unitarians? Good youth, it is most certainly out of the suburbs. As the chicken issueth from the egg, the frog from the pool, the crocodile from the Nile, and the black man from the tropics, so issueth Nonconformity from the suburbs.

I am a Nonconformist myself, and would fain speak no evil of my kind; and it is not wicked to rehearse broad facts. Yet I could wish that Nonconformity were not quite so suburban as it really is. I believe that Cromwell, and Hampden, and Andrew Marvel, and the Pilgrim Fathers, and

John Wesley, and the Rev. Mr. Kilham, must all have been suburbans in a quiet way. And I have never doubted for a moment that the Rev. R. J. Campbell, the Rev. Sylvester Horne, the Rev. Dr. Clifford, the Rev. Dr. Nicoll, the Rev. General Booth, and the Rev. Gipsy Smith, not to mention plain lay Mr. Perks, are suburbans of the suburbans. This is regrettable, because, when all is said, if Nonconformity could only get rid of its suburban drone, its suburban aims, its suburban waffing of the arms and flourishing of the napkin, and its suburban lust for publicity and notoriety, there might be some hope for it.

Against the arrogance and insolence of Churchmen and the intolerance of Churchmen it is every man's duty to rebel. Spiritual authority will always be spiritual authority, and a power before which one may expediently bow one's crested and independent head; but when spiritual authority begins too palpably to arrogate to itself a temporal and material pragmatism, it is surely high time for us to nonconform.

And how shall we best set about it? Suburbia,

the excellent, unblemished, feather-headed Suburbia, has shown us the way, and read out the lesson for us in no uncertain tones. Imprimis, we must build tin chapels, and chapels of thrifty brick, and chapels with niggard stone fronts, and chapels with toy towers and spires; item, we must make 'a leading feature' of young people's meetings and tea-meetings, and mothers' meetings, and Pleasant Sunday Afternoons, enlivened, of course, with rag sales and bazaars and magic-lantern entertainments; item, we must have organ-playings, and fiddle-scrapings, and cornet-blowings, and mixed choirs with soloists, and services of song; item, we must dispense with ritual, and go in bald-headed for a brisk, bright, brotherly, and bravura treatment of the forms of worship; item, at a pinch we may cease to preach from the Word, and hang our discourses upon the teaching of the latest sensational novel or the paradoxical utterances of the hare-brained gentlemen with red ties who write for the *Daily News;* item, we do not require preachers or pastors, but, rather, elocutionists, and mummers, and mountebanks, and pulpiteer politicians who can draw crowds and frighten Mr. Balfour.

This is the suburban Nonconformist programme, and it is being pushed and insisted upon, and worked out to its bitterest and most searching conclusions wherever two or three suburbans are met together. It is a programme of unreason and bigotry and flat-footedness, unspirituality and darkness. It is a programme which has produced the R. J. Campbells and Dr. Cliffords and Mr. Perkses of this world, or, in other words, the Christian motorist, the Christian marabout, and the Christian organizer of million-pound funds. It has made possible, and even necessary, every species of secular byplay under the guise and in the name of religion. The Nonconformists, and each particular sect of them, have played down to Suburbia with all their souls and with all their might.

Suburbia has a peculiarly tetchy religious temperament. It is easily moved, and highly sentimental and emotional, and the numbers of it are as of the sands of the sea. On the whole, it is also short of money, credulous, fond of the meretricious, and disposed always to take religious geese for swans. A worldly-wise Nonconformity has handled it with great edification and advantage, and so long as there is Suburbia left it will continue so to be handled.

At the present moment the suburbans are rent and racked and all agog because of a simple Education Act, and quite half of them have gone over to a mad faction which does not approve of that Act, and swears by a species of social rebellion which it calls Passive Resistance.

I do not believe for a single moment that there is a Nonconformist or other person in all Suburbia that can put his hand on his heart and say that the workings of that Act have not been, or are not, wholly beneficial, or that they have created the smallest hardship among any section of the people. Yet Passive Resistance—that is to say, a flat refusal to contribute to the general expense of free secular education throughout the country—is a far deeper and more lively concern among

Nonconformists to-day than Nonconformity itself. Indeed, there are reasons for believing that this same Passive Resistance, instead of being a spontaneous agitation induced by the outraging of a great principle, is nothing more nor less than an artifice seized by the leaders of a drooping and apathetic congregation, with a view to the rehabilitation of themselves in the public eye.

Certainly Nonconformity has taken a sort of new lease of life since Passive Resistance was sprung upon it by its lion-hearted champions. Never for many years have it and they figured so prominently in the public prints, or received so much attention and deference at the hands of the powers that be. Mr. Balfour, at one point in the proceedings, is said actually to have consulted the Rev. R. J. Campbell, in the hope of some sort of a compromise being effected. Imagine the late Lord Salisbury, or, for that matter, the late Lord Beaconsfield, consulting with any such person! Nonconformity has not been at all accustomed to this kind of consideration, and, being a somewhat sad and pompous affair, the attention of the press and of Mr. Balfour and others have served only to puff it out and make it bigger and more important and more portentous in its own over-excited imagination.

Despite the gentle fomentations of the principal conspirators, however, Passive Resistance will scarcely last for ever, and when it fails completely, and dies the death to which it is foredoomed, the firebrands who originated it will most likely be at some loss to discover a new shibboleth. And at that juncture Nonconformity must look to itself if it desires to remain in the figure and likeness of a live and virile force.

The pranks that Suburbia has been allowed to play with it will not tend in the long-run to the strengthening of its loins or the hardening of its front. The whole system of by-issues and side-shows and ridiculous adventitiousness which has been tolerated in the past few decades will have to be swept away, otherwise Nonconformity must succumb, or at best decline into an effete and worn-out movement pretty similar in weakness and futility to its own precious political party, yclept, if you please, the Liberal party.

It seems possible that the day of reform is even now gone past. The man who would attempt to stem the flowing tide of suburbanism which has been allowed to flood every nook and corner of the Nonconformist camp would be indeed a brave fellow. There is nobody among the present Nonconformist leaders who possesses a tithe of the grit requisite for such a task. Will the time bring forth the man? And when he is brought forth, will Campbell, Clifford, Nicoll, Meyer, and Company refrain from slaying and casting him into the pit? We can only wait and watch.

CHAPTER XIV

SHOPS

As the gifts of chaffering, huckstering, cheapening, bartering, and general trading are purely suburban in their essence, it seems natural that the arid kingdom of Suburbia should more or less bristle with shops. To keep a shop is a suburban ideal, to buy at a shop, or, in the chaste cant of the time, to go 'shopping,' is a popular suburban amusement. Sound people insist upon their tradesmen waiting upon them; the stupid and barbarian suburbans wait upon their tradesmen.

All the shop-windows that ever were have been pranked, tricked out, decked, and dressed for the attraction of children and suburbans. A fine window display traps the suburban in precisely the same manner that a piece of cheese traps the fatuous mouse, or as the candle entices the foolish moth. The modern tradesman knows this, and spreads his lures accordingly.

Perhaps there is nothing less edifying in a world of unedifying things than the shop-windows of Suburbia. You may examine scores of them, window after window, without coming across a single cheerful indication. The entire gist of them is cheapness, with its inevitable concomitant of nastiness. Take the suburban shop of gold to start with. In the first place, you shall perceive that it does not really contain enough of the authentic metal to gild a weather-cock. There are gold rings, hall-marked, at five shillings apiece; there are fat gold watches, hall-marked, at thirty shillings apiece; there are gold sleeve-links at three and sixpence a pair, and guinea gold wedding-rings at half a guinea. The shopman, and the vast armies of manufacturers for Suburbia at the back of him, have but one notion in their tired minds, and that is to get the vastest amount of glitter and ostentation out of the minutest amount of gold. Tawdriness, glassiness, imitation, and meretriciousness are the only wear for Suburbia. It is so in pretty well all other kinds of shops—furniture shops, upholstery shops, drapers' shops, tailors' shops, and even chemists and confectioners' shops included. You can buy a suite of artistic parlour furniture in mahogany and leather, or walnut and saddle-bags, at these establishments for a five-pound note. You take it home and sit upon it, and wonder in your silly suburban mind what is the matter with it ever after. Within a year's time it begins to creak and waggle and let you down; in two years' time there is next to nothing of it left, and you sally forth to replace it, braced up with the knowledge that parlour suites are now going for the unholy sum of four pounds ten. Carpets twenty yards square for a pound; brass bedsteads, with spring mattresses thrown in, for two pounds; three-and-elevenpenny book-racks; eighteen-and-sixpenny overmantles; real oil-paintings in massive gilt frames for a guinea apiece; wicker chairs, bamboo tables and flower-stands, veneered bookcases, ivory-white wardrobes, and marble-topped dressing-tables, at Heaven alone knows what preposterous prices, all find a place in the suburban purview of things purchasable. And, to crown everything, the suburban revels in boxes of soap at three tablets for fourpence ha'penny, in indisputable eau de Cologne at a shilling a pint bottle, old English lavender-water at sixpence a pint, three-three tooth-brushes, fifty pills for tenpence ha'penny, and the like abominations. At his confectioner's there are ha'penny buns, tartlets, cheese-cakes, and sponge-cakes galore; iced biscuits at sixpence ha'penny a pound, and wildernesses of sweetmeats at four ounces for three-ha'pence.

What more could the suburban heart wish for? And who but the suburban would cast acquisitive eyes on any such goods?

Perhaps the most preposterous institution under the sun, however, is the suburban stationer's shop. Here you shall come across everything that is undesirable and mediocre, from bad pens to worse books, all for sale on unheard-of terms. In the book department you may make sure of finding, in stately half-crown rows or in indecent sixpenny piles, the vapidest literature that mortal man has indited. I dare not mention the names of the authors whose works fill up the odd corners of the fancy-goods and curl-paper repositories of Suburbia. They are a people to themselves, and well below what is considered bottom-level in the most ordinary book-shops.

As for drapers' shops, it is only in accordance with the fitness of things that, as Suburbia is largely a woman's affair, they should cumber the ground in solid rows. Here, of course, cheapness and flaringness and vulgarity run riot. Our new spring dress goods, our bankrupt stock of laces, our mantle and fur departments, our household linen departments, our stock of silks, satins, velvets, and velveteens, our haberdashery show-rooms—in fact, all sections of us, from floor to ceiling, and from No. 121 to 129, are tarred with precisely the same suburban brush, and there is not one of us that does not in some sort dazzle or delude you with the odd farthing.

Why are these dainty pocket-handkerchiefs

priced at threepence three-farthings each? Simply because we know that you have a suburban soul, and that you imagine yourself to be compassing a fourpenny article at a farthing off, whereas in point of fact the honest selling price of the goods is twopence ha'penny. Why these frequent sellings-off? these markings-down of prices? these enormous sacrifices? these salvage sales? They are designed and invented simply to tickle and satisfy your suburban maw, and we laugh in our sleeves while we flourish them in front of you.

Trade and barter, you may take it, are come to their lowest and most ignominious end in Suburbia, and this, not so much because of the wicked predilections of trade and barter, but because of the grasping and vulgar spirit which is known to permeate the soul of the suburbans.

In a sense, it would be a distinct gain if the great majority of suburban shops could be shut up, and their places taken by substantial, unpretentious warehouses. For the glitter and glare, the marble and the gilt, the parquetry floors, the elegant appointments, the smart porters, the cash railways, the perky and courteous assistants, and the aristocratic shop-walkers, Suburbia has to pay, and to pay through the nose. The two-three system looks very fine, and is no doubt one of the marvels of modern commerce, but it does not necessarily mean that you are getting value.

The best advice that one can give to the thrifty suburban who would fain go shopping in his or her own district is—DON'T. Or if you do, frequent only the old-fashioned establishments, which decline to be bothered with farthings. Truly, such establishments are becoming few and far between, but there is here and there such an one left, and you ought to deal with it, even if you lose money and get a less variegated choice for your pains. Suburban shops in the main and of the ruck are to be eschewed. One can come to no possible good in them, and until they mend their ways, and cast two-three and all that it means to the winds, one should steadfastly pass them by.

CHAPTER XV

ARCHITECTURE

It seems more than probable that the benightedness of Suburbia in the mass is largely the outcome of the slackness and unimaginativeness of architects. I suppose that British architecture as a whole was never in a more parlous state than it is to-day. Go where you will, whether in England or Scotland, it is the architecture of the past that is serious and dignified and satisfying, and the architecture of the present that is trivial, paltry, and annoying. Even when you give the modern architect unlimited opportunities in the way of site and money, he usually succeeds in making a botch of it.

Examples will occur to the minds of everybody who cares to reflect for a moment. In this place, however, we are more particularly concerned with the architects of Suburbia, and there can be no doubt whatever that their handiwork proves them to be a most sorry lot. Like a good many other professional persons, they appear to be convinced that it is necessary for them to truckle to their suburban patrons, and they have truckled and bowed and scraped with a vengeance. *Ad captandum vulgus* applies just as much in architecture as in any other art.

For the wealthy, bloated, bourgeois person it is possible to build a house that will make him purr with delight, and yet be an outrage and an insult to the decent eye. This has been achieved times without number by architects who esteem themselves artists, and consider the painter and the sculptor to be merely their peers. When the architect looks on Suburbia, it is plain that he has for it that eye of contempt which is encouraged by all other sorts and conditions of men. He conceives that Suburbia cannot possibly require what is comely and worthy and pleasant, but only what is showy and garish and cheap.

And he goes to work in that wise. After years of fiddling, experiment, calculation, and feeling about, he has evolved, for example, a type of house of from £50 to £80 a year rental, which, while it exactly suits Suburbia and represents the very height of convenience from the point of view of suburban landlord and tenants alike, is nevertheless an abomination before the Lord. I refer to the bay-windowed villa of six rooms and a bathroom, with a sort of lean-to annexe at the back, and the scrubbiest and least ample piece of palisaded garden in front. These houses have been erected by the thousand in mean, unchristian rows wherever there is a suburb. A very large section of the population of Suburbia is destined to live in them all its life. They are poky, narrow, skimpy, oppressive, and foully dear at the money.

A noticeable and irritating fact about them is that they are always arranged and fitted in such a manner that they can be let off in two portions; that is to say, the tenant takes the whole house, and is at liberty to let half of it for such moneys as he can get. This system may be very useful in assisting landlords and estate-agents to any number of tenants, but it is subversive of the best interests of domesticity. An Englishman's house should be his castle; it should not be infested by any other family save his own. There can be no real domesticity, no real domestic hearth, no sufficient domestic government, no adequate domestic seclusion and independence, where you have two or more families under one roof.

Suburbia has suffered immeasurable evil through this principle of one house two families, while the landlords and the estate exploiters have filled their greedy pockets out of it. Of course, the excuse is that the population of London has become so enormous that families must be stacked one on top of the other or remain homeless. In point of fact, however, this is no excuse at all. Suburbia has always been noted for its snobbish insistence on appearances. It may be earning a hundred and fifty a year, but it will not be happy unless it can make pretence that its income runs to three hundred a year. When one snob suburban takes

'Heatherfield,' that most desirable semi-detached villa, salubriously situated, one minute from bus, tram, and three stations, he is well aware that the rent of the place, with taxes very generously thrown in, is entirely beyond him; but he is also well aware that he will not have vast difficulty in finding another snob suburban who will pay him hard money for the pleasure of sharing with him the glories and conveniences of 'Heatherfield.' Both of them print 'Heatherfield' on their limp cards, both of them print 'Heatherfield' on their high-falutin note-paper, and when themselves and their wives die, 'Heatherfield' will be found engraved on their bumptious little suburban hearts.

To look down the terrace in which 'Heatherfield' is situated is to be transformed at once into a morose, black-speck-seeing, bilious pessimist. For not only is there 'Heatherfield,' but there are also 'Daisyfield,' 'Gladysfield,' 'Rosefield,' 'Greenfield,' and even 'Beaconsfield,' good honest Arabic numerals being at a distinct discount for putting up on houses in Suburbia.

And the horrible part about it is that all these pretentious, paper-walled, ruddle-faced, glassy-eyed residences, fifty or more of them on either side of the terrace, are absolutely, preternaturally, and scandalously the counterpart of each other. The sameness and triteness and grinning undelightfulness of it all is bound to be reflected in the character and habits, and even in the physique, of that terrace's population. The men are as like one another as peas; the women are as like one another as peas; the children are the children of one quarrelsome, stingy, money-grubbing, undistinguished family.

The people are dwellers in half-houses to a soul. They are born wranglers over garden walls and reproachers of one another on staircases. There is a grievance raging somewhere in every single breast of them. Mrs. Tumpkins imagines that the bathroom and the washhouse are hers, and hers alone. 'I pay my rent, and I have as much right to the bathroom and the washhouse as Mrs. Wilkins has, even if she is the landlady.' 'Brown thinks that, because he pays me his measly fourteen shillings a week for the upstairs half of "Rosefield," he, Brown, is supreme in this house. But, my dear, it is I, Jones, who am master, it is I who am the householder, and responsible for rent, rates, and taxes; and if I do not give Brown notice to quit on Saturday my name is not what it is.' And so on and so forth.

Half of it, at any rate, is blamable on the architects, who should certainly be ashamed of themselves. But, of course, an architect can never bring himself to regard a suburban house in a spiritual sense, otherwise his chances of becoming really eminent in his profession would be gone for ever.

And when you call him in on the shop business, or on the assembly-rooms business, or on the music-hall and theatre business, or, for that matter, on the chapel and church business, what does he do for you? Well, he panders unblushingly to your lowest and most brutish suburban instincts. He offers you the grossest and crassest of edifices, and rings the changes on suburban mediocrities, with a fiendish disregard for everything in the world but his own immediate profit. You are a suburban; he knows exactly what is likely to meet with your ill-conditioned approval, and he gives it to you, with his blessing and hypocritical and sycophantic remarks as to your excellent taste. If you were a Hottentot or an Australian black fellow, he would provide you with plans for kraals and brushwood huts with the same dispassionate hand and with the same dishonest compliments. It is the architect who has made the ugly face of Suburbia ugly beyond tolerance; it is the architect who has made it preposterous beyond preposterousness; it is the architect whose cheek ought to flame, and whose liver ought to wither, at the sight of it all.

CHAPTER XVI

HORTICULTURE

WE HAVE it on the best of authority that a love of flowers is a true sign of gentle birth and reasonable breeding. It is possibly for this reason that the suburbans of all degrees do their best to secure some sort of an apology for a garden at the back or front of their houses. Indeed, one may assert with safety that suburban gardens are of two kinds, namely—front and back.

And first as to front-gardens. These, though obviously intended for show, like front-windows and front-curtains, are nine times out of ten of a very narrow and circumscribed area, consisting, in fact, of a few square feet of turf with a circular flower-bed in the middle of it. But narrow and cramped though the ground at disposal may be, the suburbans exhibit a preternatural ingenuity in the diversity of their treatment of it. In fact, though you may find a terrace or avenue of a hundred houses all as like each other as copper pennies, and all with precisely the same area of garden, you shall discover on examination that each of those gardens is an individual concern, and differs from its neighbours in the most marked manner. This is largely because suburban horticulturists are pretty vague both as to the theory and practice of the art in which they delight. The great majority of them, unfortunately, put their faith in penny packets of seed and fine hardy geraniums at three-ha'pence the pot. When you sow a pennyworth of seeds, or from that to a shilling's-worth in Suburbia, you can never be quite sure as to what will eventually come up.

There are the cats to consider, and the sparrows, and the children, and the moral obliquity of the seedsman. Which latter, in the full knowledge that he is serving mere Suburbia, takes his risk, and hands out whatever may happen to be stirring, with small regard to accuracy about sorts. To take an instance in point, his pennyworth of mignonette seed may result in the effloration on your circular plot of a fine crop of variegated poppies. But by the time these have bloomed you are really incapable of remembering what it was that you asked for, and if you complained the seedsman would inquire dulcetly whether you expected to acquire Kew Gardens, with the floral side of Hyde Park thrown in, for a penny. In the main, however, the seed you sow usually yields nasturtiums of the feeblest and least convincing yellow hue, despite the fact that you may have ordered German asters, double stocks, lily of the valley, dahlias, or blue tulip. As for the geraniums in pots, they are a timid, desultory, and disappointing growth.

You may keep them in the pots if you be so minded, and water them with great and unfailing regularity. The result varies, but it is wise to assume beforehand that it will amount to three leaves and a flake of bloom on a sort of cabbage-stalk of wood. If, on the other hand, you plant your geraniums out, they die that same evening or get stolen by little boys.

On the whole, therefore, you are pushed by force of circumstance in the direction of shell or cork rockeries and ferns. Many delightful evenings may be spent in the intelligent building up and disposition of these horticultural marvels. The shell of the succulent escallop and the juicy oyster, saved from supper or purchased by the brown-paper-bag-full from under a stall, comes in most handily for your purpose. If you prefer cork, you can purchase it in bundles at any respectable florist's.

Having secured material, you set to work to create, as it were. And you need never be ashamed of your handiwork, because the householder next door is, as a rule, possessed of less taste and decidedly less shell or cork than yourself. Go at it with a will, dear friend, give a free rein to your suburban fancy and imagination; so shall you produce something that cats will howl over by night, and that sharp terriers and flingers of orange-peel will desecrate by day. The ferns, of course, come later, and inasmuch as your garden lacks shade, or, haply, has a glaring southern frontage, they make a point of going early. In the long-run you resign yourself to the plain brown-green turf and simple, cropless, rain-beaten, soot-sprinkled, earthy, circular flower-bed, with absolutely nothing in it, saving, perhaps, a dingy flat chip, marked in well-nigh undecipherable plumbago, 'Nasturtiums.'

Now, back-gardens, as luck will have it, are slightly different. Commonly they are of greater expanse than their fellows of the front; commonly they rejoice in a more ample measure of seclusion. There are high walls round them, or a wooden fence. There is room for a walk and a trellis-arch or so. If you are a suburban of parts, you can divide them up into lawn and flower-beds, with a small kitchen-garden beyond.

And here, of course, you are at liberty to delve with greater assiduity, and to sow and plant with greater security, though you still have to contend, perforce, with the cats, the sparrows, and the children of your next-door neighbours. In the spring you may raise coarse grass, crocuses, and daffodils, which latter, you will find on reference to your favourite classic, Shakespeare,

> 'Come before the swallow dares, and take
> The winds of March with beauty.'

The fact that in Suburbia there are no swallows, and that March is usually a muggy, placid, sooty month, is a mere detail.

After the crocuses and the daffodils you must depend once again on the never-failing nasturtium. It makes a brave show of green and orange on the wall-sides, and it clambers over your trellis-arch with singular agility.

In the autumn, I am afraid, there is nothing for you but potted geraniums, dubious ferns, and shell or cork rockeries; while in the winter, of course, you go out of the horticultural business altogether, and spread your back-garden with crumbs for the birds, and cutlet bones and broken victuals for your own dog and an occasional stray cat. Adam was a gardener, and so are you. But what a difference! I am touched and ravished by your pathetic primeval desires in horticultural directions, and yet neither of us can help admitting that the outcome of them is legitimate matter for smiling.

The fact is that the soul of you and the suburbanism of you absolutely prohibit and render impossible anything in the shape of effective horticultural pursuits. You can no more make real gardens in Suburbia than you can play billiards at sea. Your only way out is to purchase lavishly at the cabbage stalls and the cut-flower stalls. Your stomach helps you to the one, and your stinginess and sneaking regard for Post-Office Savings Banks debars you from the other. Besides, what in the name of goodness should you really want with flowers, or flowers with you? If you were an honest flowerful person, you would forego and disavow your suburbanisn. But as such renunciation and disavowal are impossible to you, why worry? Horticulture in the suburbs, like most other things in the suburbs, is a fiction and a pretence. Let us leave it at that.

CHAPTER XVII

THE GREAT SERVANT QUESTION

It has been arranged by Providence that the female population of Suburbia should always be in more or less of a state of agitation about its servants. The complaint that servants are 'so dreadful, my dear,' is a purely suburban one. You never hear a woman of position whining because she cannot get exactly what she wants out of her maids. In point of fact, she gets exactly what she wants and what she pays for—namely, due and efficient service and civility.

The real reason why servants are so dreadful in Suburbia is because, nine times out of ten, they belong to the same class as their mistresses, who, not to put too fine a point upon it, were born to wrestle, not to reign. Also, as a rule, they get meted out to them treatment which would make a brass knocker rebel. The average suburban mistress of servants is always either a feather-headed, foolish, inept person or a common natterer and scold. If she be the former, it is only to be expected that Mary Jane or Flossie, as the case may be, should get somewhat out of hand. The mistress who gossips with you, and giggles with you, and discusses her private affairs with you, and generally treats you for all the world as though you were her sister, seldom commands your respect; and it is scarcely your fault if you serve her in a somewhat perfunctory, haphazard, and uncertain way. And at times, when she displeases you, you are surely quite within your rights if you give her a piece of your mind. She may weep passionate tears, and give you notice, with sobs, in consequence; but you know that the affair will soon blow over, that the victory will be yours, and that every such difference really strengthens your position.

As for master, poor man! he is seldom at

home. If he had an inkling of what was going on, he would wax irascible, and he might even swear. As it is, you are civility itself when he addresses you, and he is of opinion that you are a remarkably smart and well-intentioned servant.

Of course, I need scarcely say that your real troubles begin when you happen to fall into a household where the lady is a bit of a tartar—one of those persistent, acid, and bitter tartars in which Suburbia appears to abound. This good woman usually succeeds in inflicting upon you unthinkable sufferings and privations.

First of all she insists upon lugging you out of bed at six-thirty a.m. sharp, and this winter and summer, if you please. Nobody about her domicile even dreams of stirring until eight or eight-thirty of the clock, but it is the duty of a good 'general' to be up with the lark—or, in other words, the alarum—and up you have to get. Then, of course, from the time of your rising to the time of your going to bed you must needs be kept on the run, not because there is a great deal to do, but because it is the duty of a good 'general' with £15 a year, and all found, to run. Further, the admirable supervisor of your destinies is very keen on the food question. She locks everything away from you, doles out your every meal with a stingy hand, and keeps a special and peculiar brand of butter, bacon, eggs, sugar, and so forth, which are quite good enough for servants.

Then there is the question of followers and of evenings out. Mrs. Scold will not have followers at any price, and evenings out mean, with her, one evening a month, and a short evening at that. You go out at six, if you can get off, and you must be in again at ten to the tick. She is not going to have her house turned into a rendezvous, whatever that may mean. So that on the whole your life in such a service is a weariness and an annoyance, and you spend the best part of it wishing your mistress anywhere but where she is, and making up your mind to get a new place.

On the other hand, ghastly tales reach one from time to time as to the inborn foolishness and wickedness of the suburban servant herself. I am told that as a rule she is a helpless, thoughtless, uncultivated, depraved creature, indolent to the backbone, devoted to dirt, slatternliness, and muddle, and seldom or never worth her salt. It is she who spends three-quarters of an hour and a quart of paraffin on the lighting of a single fire. It is she who never can manage to crawl downstairs till long after the milk has been and the postman has rapped. It is she whose kettles never boil, whose bacon and eggs are burnt black, whose tea is a murderous potion, whose boiled eggs are as hard as money-lenders' hearts, whose washings and scrubbings and sweepings and dustings touch merely the surface of things, who cannot boil a potato or cook a shoulder of mutton, who has no notion of punctuality or regularity or the deference due to her betters, and whose appetite, pardie, rivals in persistence and comprehensibility that of the famous dragon of Wantley. It is she also who devotes so many half-hours every day to the cultivation of polite conversation with butchers, bakers, dustmen, and other callers.

It is she who can be depended upon to be an unconscionably long time gone if you send her on an errand, and whose great aim in life is to become engaged to the policeman, who eats your mutton and drinks your beer, and marry him under your nose.

There may be truth in all this, or it may be the profoundest slander; but suburban mistresses will subscribe to every word of it, and might, an they would, tell us a good deal more that is even less creditable to the suburban Mary Jane. One thing is certain, however, that, either through faults on either one side or the other, suburban mistresses are continually changing servants.

At the registry-offices you can hear fearsome tales of mistresses who never keep a servant more than a fortnight, and of servants who never stay in a place more than ten days. And I am disposed to think that both parties have latterly become so inured to mutation that they feel rather aggrieved if the necessity for a swift and acrimonious parting fails to arise.

The attitude of mind which says, 'There is a new servant in the house; I don't suppose she'll suit me,' or 'I suppose this place is sure to be like the last, namely, a dog-hole,' is not, after all, the right attitude, and it certainly does not conduce to a good understanding or lengthy employment. Mistresses and servants alike are too prone to arrive at hasty conclusions about one another. Hence their failure to agree.

I think, too, the servant question owes not a little of its perennialness in Suburbia to the fact that, when Suburban women meet, they are usually at a loss for subjects of conversation, and fall back on servants, just as suburban men fall back on the weather. I have heard a female suburban, who was blessed with an absolutely faithful and immaculate cook and 'general,' run down the whole tribe of handmaidens with a bitterness and asperity that approached the marvellous. Indeed, it is the fashion among suburban mistresses to asperse servants, just as it is the fashion among suburban servants to asperse and cry 'old cat' over their mistresses.

I am afraid that the plain truth is that the great majority of persons who keep servants in Suburbia do not really need to keep them at all. In a reasonable household servants are employed because they are a necessity. In too many suburban households, on the other hand, servants are a superfluity and an ostentation.

It would seem that the authentic and proper servitors of Suburbia should not hail from a registry-office, or be recognised members of the noble army of servant-girls at all. Rather should they consist of a brawny charwoman and a limp little step-girl. In the suburban organs of light and leading the advertisements of such unattached retainers abound. Suburbia employs them by the thousand, and rewards them with the meagrest of pittances. They have their faults and their drawbacks, like most other human institutions, but, on the whole, they are as admirably suited to the needs and requirements of Suburbia as Suburbia is suited to them.

CHAPTER XVIII

THE THEATRE

TIME was when the suburbs did not possess a theatre wherewithal to bless themselves. Within the last decade or so, however, theatrical managers have discovered that the mountain may with advantage be established on the doorstep of Mahomet. The country of Suburbia nowadays bristles with theatres, all of them brand-new, spick and span, and organized on the most approved principles, and all of them engaged in the provision of that peculiar species of theatrical entertainment in which the suburban soul delights. Of course, the British drama as an institution is largely a suburban affair in itself. It has existed for many years on the patronage of middling and suburban people, and it is for middling and suburban people that its leading lights make a point of catering. So that when your suburban theatres are once built there is precious little difficulty in supplying them with the right fare. Anything that can be staged with success in London proper may be depended upon to meet with the enthusiastic approval and the generous support of the suburbs. Furthermore, many a foolish and gauche piece of dramatic writing which London proper declines to patronize at any price finds in the suburbs respectful and enthusiastic admiration.

While, of course, the theatrical entertainment provided for suburban audiences is, on the whole, sloppy and commonplace, both as regards matter and manner, there cannot be the slightest doubt that suburban audiences are beginning to be recognised at their true worth by the great unacted and the equally great uncast. If you have a play which the managers of London decline flatly to touch, even with a pair of tongs, 'put it on' yourself at a suburban theatre, and you may come out winner after all. On the other hand, if you are a mute, inglorious Romeo, or Hamlet, or Othello, or Shylock, or Whatshisname in 'The Bells,' and you cannot get the haughty entrepreneurs of the chief city of the world to furnish forth for you that chance which is alone wanted to bring you into immediate line with Garrick, Macready, Irving, and Mr. Beerbohm Tree, again you will be well advised if you confine yourself to the suburbs.

I am not aware that there are too many particular instances in point; but so far as plays are concerned, I think that the immortal works of Mr. George Bernard Shaw have received a good deal more attention from suburban audiences than they have from the audiences of London proper. Possibly the Coronet Theatre, where Mr. Shaw's chiefest triumphs appear to have been achieved, does not quite call itself a suburban theatre. But it is pretty far out, anyway, and I have seen it pretty full of snobs on more than one occasion. And when I say snobs, I mean Bayswater snobs, who, as everybody is aware, are the primest on this globe of sinful contrarients.

In a sense this is unfortunate for Mr. George Bernard Shaw, and it throws a curious light on the mind of suburbia. If Mr. Shaw had been told a couple of years back that he would find his first real recognition among the suburbans, he would no doubt have shouted in a loud and terrible voice, 'Perish the thought!' Life, however, is largely a matter of ironies, and Mr. Shaw must put up with the kind of appreciation he can get, even if it be only suburban. I have a suspicion, however, that Mr. Shaw need not plume himself too greatly over his ostensible successes. Suburbia laughs at his plays, pleasant or unpleasant as the case may be; but does it really understand them?

For myself I have grave doubts on the subject. You may take it for an axiom that your true suburban makes a point of laughing and weeping at the right places. If you tell him that such and such a 'piece' is a screaming farce, the suburban will do his best to scream for you, strong in the knowledge that a screaming farce is a thing to be screamed at; if, on the other hand, you assure him that your dramatic work is a touching, tender, and exquisitely pathetic piece of writing, goodman Suburb will blubber over it for you with the best.

Broadly speaking, his ideal comic author is Mr. Jerome K. Jerome, and when he wants a little pathos he has a habit of turning to the weepier productions of Dr. J. M. Barrie. In so far as any writer, dramatic or otherwise, under the sun approaches or resembles these shining ideals, in so far will he become popular in Suburbia.

Now, while there is a great deal in Mr. Shaw's comedies which may be reckoned altogether witty and profound, there is also in them a loose and quasi-humorous quality, which for want of a better term may be called J. K. Jeromey. And it seems to me possible that it is precisely this quality, and no other, which has drawn Suburbia to Mr. Shaw. Perhaps I am mistaken, but I don't like to think so.

With regard to actors, the suburbans would appear to be agreed that there are only two great actors on the English stage, the names of them being Beerbohm Tree and G. P. Huntley. Mr. Tree's genius has always gone unquestioned in Suburbia. He has a manner and tastes and methods which appeal irresistibly to suburban susceptibilities. In this place I shall pass upon him no strictures.

Of Mr. G. P. Huntley, a gentleman who, as it seems to me, is possessed of an admirable suburban point of view, has lately written as follows:

'Mr. Huntley's place in London's warm heart has been won, I imagine, by a gift of ordered imbecility, fortified by the manner of the tired swell and a rich "society" drawl. These make his superficial appeal; but one soon perceives that he has more beneath. He has tact; amid all the foolishness and all the crude impossibility of this play (if play is the word), he keeps his head, and, what is stranger, his dignity. He has fun and he has radiance. But above all he has charm. Charm is very rare, as one discovers on sitting down to make a list of the actors who have it. But Mr. Huntley certainly is one of them. . . .

Suddenly, perhaps in the act of laughing in the ordinary way at an ordinary idiocy, one is conscious that here are the makings of a fine actor—here, indeed, is a fine actor; that here is a man capable of compelling an audience not only to laugh, but to cry, too, just as he wished. It is all irresponsibility at present, and I understand always has been; but I believe that if Mr. Huntley had a human part he could play it wonderfully.'

One need scarcely say that no suburban worth the name would quarrel with this appraisement. In fairness it should be added that the appraiser is himself a comic, being part-author of no less a masterpiece than 'Wisdom while you Wait,' and that he has asserted elsewhere that 'ladies are all ticklish,' and that the best comic song in the world is Mr. Harry Lauder's 'Stop your tickling, Jock.'

We may here conveniently say our say as to suburban music-halls. The music-hall is, on the face of it, even a more suburban affair than the theatre. Before there were any music-halls in the suburbs that counted, the music-hall was still suburban. So that the scattering of 'Palaces' and 'Empires' and suchlike among the gay suburbs has been, as it were, a simple matter of turning again home. The new order of things saves tram and train fares, and Suburbia rejoices therefor. Also two shows a night, a steady run of stars, and no waiting, please the suburban to the marrow of his bones. Withal, the programmes put forward are pretty much what music-hall programmes usually have been—a bringing together of the sheerest, gaudiest, most glittering, and most foolish vulgarities. One cannot be sure, despite the unquestionable 'convenience' of having a music-hall within the gate, so to speak, that the fact of such possession is an unmixed blessing.

When people with a music-hall turn of mind were compelled to seek their pleasure in mid-London, the time and costs of journeying to and fro acted as a sort of deterrent against over-indulgence. Nowadays the suburban music-hall-lover can provide himself with entertainment at about a fourth of the old expense. So that he can afford to indulge his passion four times a week instead of once, as formerly. And this, I should surmise, is eminently bad for him, tending, indeed, to confirm him in the least lovely of his suburban idiosyncrasies. However, the music-hall has arrived, and it looks like staying. Master and Miss Subub must therefore take their chance.

CHAPTER XIX

CHAMBER MUSIC

THERE'S not the smallest orb which thou behold'st, but in his motion like an angel sings, still quiring to the young-eyed cherubins! And there is not the smallest suburb in all Suburbia which does not, to use its own phrase, 'go in' for music. Suburban music, of course, is principally of one kind—that is to say, it is piano music. The pianos from which it is extorted are also of one kind—namely, cheap and tinkly.

I suppose that to a person whose ear is properly attuned to the finer species of sound the music of Suburbia must be well-nigh intolerable. Indeed, it seems to consist of a perpetual practising of scales, and a fingering out of 'Every Morn I bring thee Violets.' It is chamber music with the chamber very much insisted upon. It consists of homely, simple, domestic tunes, such as might delight the soul of Mr. William Archer, or Mr. Alexander of 'Glory Song' fame. It is music which, somehow, always has a cross over the notes suitable for the thumb, and 1, 2, 3, or 4 over the notes suitable for the fingers. It is music which is in a perpetual state of cultivation, but never seems to get any forrader. It is sentimental music, inasmuch as it makes a great show with 'The Old Folks at Home,' 'Daddy,' 'Where is my Wandering Boy To-night?' 'Skylark, Skylark,' and similar incomparable airs; and it is loyal music, because it invariably insists upon 'God save the King,' or parts of it, three or four times in the course of a single sitting.

Of course, I speak here of suburban music in the mass or flood. There be musicianers in Suburbia who stand out of the ruck, and dote upon Wagner. And these, perhaps, are really the worst sort, because quite frequently they are a distinct source of annoyance, not only to those who dwell in the house with them, but to the neighbours. A suburban Wagnerite might appear at first blush to be a contradiction in terms, but in point of fact there are great numbers of them. The fame of Richard, not to say the blare of him, has penetrated into the dark and the void, and he has become a suburban cult, even if he be not a suburban popular favourite. Easy arrangements of a wedding march of his are in steady demand in Crouch End music-shops, and at Hampstead and Surbiton full scores of him can always be obtained for you—to order.

There are people who will tell you that Wagner was as great a musician as Shakespeare was a poet. With such people I make it a point to agree to differ, and I think that Wagner's reputation among the suburbans justifies me in so doing. For whatever the suburbans like or admire, or reach after, must have grave defects about it, must be garish and overobtrusive and uninspired —which is exactly what is the matter with Wagner.

A musician who for his proper interpretation requires an orchestra of about the size of an army corps may or may not be a tremendous fellow, but he is admirably cut out for Suburbia. Mr. Sousa's works also demand execution on biggish orchestras, and Suburbia likes Mr. Sousa.

However, these are scarcely questions for lay persons, though it is well that they should be noted. Apart from elementary piano-playing, the vamping and strumming out of tunes and Wagner, suburban music scarcely exists. The violin, it may be, is encouraged among promising children, though 'The Bluebells of Scotland' is the average limit of their attainment. There are old gentlemen in odd corners who play the flute. There are middle-aged, lymphatic gentlemen who exercise themselves occasionally on the cornet, and there are young gentlemen in spectacles who play the organs and harmoniums in churches and chapels. I have heard even of a lady in Suburbia who plucks delicately at the harp.

All the same, the suburbans come sadly short of being in any wise a musical people. At the present moment vigorous attempts are being made to remove this reproach by the introduction of the mechanical piano-player. I am told that with the help of this ingenious invention you can play anything in the world, provided you have by you the necessary spools of music. As the piano-player can be had on the hire system, and entirely disposes of the necessity for music lessons at thirteen shillings a quarter, Suburbia has taken to it like a duck takes to water.

Hence it comes to pass that you now have wafted on the air of certain terraces Chopin, Mendelssohn, Bach, Gounod, Verdi, Schumann, Rossini, and all the rest of them, whereas a few short summers ago you could hear nothing but the jigglety-jogglety Sullivan and Moody and Sankey's hymns. And yet methinks that, if Chopin or Mendelssohn or any of their peers could have foreseen that they should come to this pass, they might have refrained from composition at all.

The real musical stand-by of Suburbia is the perambulating, itinerant, green-carpet-covered piano-organ. Than this recondite instrument none is diviner. Dragged creakingly to your front-gate by a couple of grinning persons with the blood of the Cæsars in them, it takes up little room, and you can send it away forthwith if you don't happen to feel musically inclined. There is, I believe, a police by-law which enables you to do as much with impunity. But if you are a true suburban you will not send it away. Rather will you despatch your maid-of-all-work to bestow upon those grinning Latians two pennies and an odd farthing, and bid them give you as much as they can for the money, and be sure to play 'Won't you come home, Bill Bailey?' thrice over, because it hath a dying fall. And you command that handmaiden on her return straightway to open each of the front-windows, so that you may have the full benefit of the mellifluous tide in all your chambers, and lose no scruple of your legitimate twopence-farthing's-worth. Furthermore, by opening the front-windows you may, after your own particular recital is concluded, still participate in the entertainment, rewarded with a penny, by the mistress of the house a few doors further down. Indeed, until the machine works its way completely out of earshot, the sweetness of it is yours, even though it be only in a far-away, tailing-off degree.

I am disposed to set it down for an axiom, that if there had been no suburbs there had been no piano-organs. It is the suburbs, and the suburbs only, that keep Saffron Hill in revenue and render the twining of handles a profitable Italian industry. And to Suburbia be the honour and the glory!

Before I leave this part of my discourse I shall beg respectfully to ask of the suburbans a particular favour. They have their pianos and their Wagner; they have their miscellaneous instruments, from the organ right down to the hujah; they have their mechanical piano-players; and above all they have their ineffable piano-organs. What more could the heart of a good suburban, no matter how musical, desire? I think one may answer, in the name of Tubal Cain and St. Cecilia, nothing. And yet cunning, malicious, and greedy persons have contrived, and put upon the suburban market, certain blasphemous instruments with tin discs in them, which play 'Home, Sweet Home' in a box on the turning of a little handle.

Now, I am in a position to assert that these hurdy-gurdlets have found not the smallest favour in the abodes of the opulent, or, perhaps it were better to say, in the domiciles of substantial persons who are not suburbans. Neither have they been purchased in any numbers by the baser, blacker, unmoneyed rabblement—which also are not suburbans. Now and again a Vicar buys one for the behoof of a mendicant blind man, or a drunken, roistering coster takes one home in the faith that it will amuse the 'nippers.' But the real bazaar, exchange and mart for this instrument has always been and still is Suburbia. In four suburban houses out of five you can find it wheezily enthroned, and in process of being paid for at the unholy rate of a shilling a week. It plays everything by turn, and nothing long, and it plays everything wickedly. One had better be stone-deaf all one's life than listen for a moment to its blandishments. It is music with the 'm' and machine works its way completely out of earshot, the sweetness of it is yours, even though it be only in a far-away, tailing-off degree.

I am disposed to set it down for an axiom, that if there had been no suburbs there had been no piano-organs. It is the suburbs, and the suburb[illegible] only, that keep Saffron Hill in revenue a[illegible] render the twining of handles a profitable It[illegible] industry. And to Suburbia be the honour the glory!

Before I leave this part of my discourse I beg respectfully to ask of the suburbans a ticular favour. They have their pianos a[illegible] Wagner; they have their miscellaneous ments, from the organ right down to t[illegible] they have their mechanical piano-pla[illegible] above all they have their ineffable p[illegible] What more could the heart of a g[illegible] no matter how musical, desire? I [illegible] answer, in the name of Tubal Cecilia, nothing. And yet cur[illegible] and greedy persons have con[illegible] upon the suburban market, cer[illegible]

·ᴱR XX

PICTURES

..ce of mural decoration
.. the lead. She is a born
..ded they have gilt frames
. believed to have a biggish
rations of the Hanging
.al Academy. In her midst
..blishments flourish and
.een bay-trees. 'Finest stock
..dings in the district.' This is
..s up and glorifies the pictorial

..ut to purchase a picture in this
teps are bent faithfully in the
the picture-frame establishment.
r, a snuffy elderly gentleman in a

soiled apron, and with a smell of glue on him, inquires of you blandly what you might be pleased to want. When you say 'pictures,' he inquires, 'What price about?' and, 'How does this style of frame suit you?' He tells you that he is just expecting a little consignment of real old English gold mouldings which he proposes to re-do-up and issue to the public at a fabulous sacrifice. Would you like to wait till the goods come in, or shall he saw off and gild for you a few yards of this German stuff? If you persist in saying 'pictures,' he laughs feebly, and informs you that pictures are all very well, but the frame's the thing. 'What is home without a mother?' quotha, 'and what is a picture, ay, even one of your Gainsboroughs or Landseers, or Turners, or Tademas, without a frame? Why, frames are half the battle—and a good deal more than half, even at the Royal Academy itself.'

But to come down to business, what sort of pictures might you be wanting? He has a very good line in half-crown replicas in photogravure of the great anecdotal masters. 'There is them things of Rossetti's and Burne-Jones's in black polished frames, with a gilt beading complete, at three and sixpence a time.' Or would the gentleman care to invest in a little real oil-painting? Here you are—three pairs of high-class landscapes on Bristol board by Twister, signed front and back, and going cheap for the sake of clearing them out, as it is not every customer who comes into this shop what has a real eye for a picture. Twister's six *chefs d'œuvres*, framed up in the best English gilt, will run you into a paltry three guineas, with hooks to hang them up by gratis. You can take them or leave them, as there really is no profit on them. And so on and so forth. And when you, the wall-furnishing suburban, manage to rise a little above art for the frames' sake, what do you do? Well, on some muggy, drizzly December evening when you have missed your train, and have consequently twenty minutes on your hand, you drop into a street-side auction, where a heavy-moustached Hebrew has for disposal without reserve sundry boxes of cigars, sundry pieces of gold and gem jewellery, half a dozen melodeons, a child's bassinette, and some pictures. With the intuition of his race, the Hebrew perceives in the twinkling of an eye that you are a patron of the arts, a picture-buyer and a Mæcenas to boot. Wherefore he waves aside the child's bassinette, and the melodeons, and the golden gem jewellery, and the cigars.

'Tholly,' he says, 'there is a customer among us. Reach down one them mastherpieces. Now, gentlemen, how much for the mastherpiece? Warranted real oils, duly signed and authenticated by Shribson, who had four pictures in the Royal Academy last year, and is going to have a room to himself when the show opens again. How much shall we say, gentlemen? Don't all speak at once I am not selling you frames, though they are well worth the money. Shall we say a guinea? No bidders? Well, then, let's start it at fifteen bob—going at fifteen bob, fifteen bob, fifteen bob, fifteen bob for the authentic Shribson—sixteen shillings (thank you, sir), sixteen shillings, sixteen shillings and six—sixteen shillings and sixpence. Going at sixteen and sixpence—I must remind you, gentlemen, that Shribson is coming on, and that this is considered by the critics to be his best work—going at sixteen and sixpence, a real Shribson, whose father was half-brother to J. M. W. Turner—going at sixteen and sixpence (impressive silence)—gone!'

And so home to your suburb with an unwieldy, flat, brown-paper parcel under your arm, at the sight of which parcel the wife of your bosom sighs wearily: 'Oh, this art!' For, good woman, she knows full well that every sovereign you spend in the purchase of oil-paintings reduces the fund which will possibly be available for her annual trip to Bexhill or Yarmouth in the summer, and she writhes accordingly. You, on the other hand, have secured a gem and are happy.

In the face of these things, it is remarkable that in the suburbs you will find always the haunts and homes of our principal British artists. St. John's Wood, for example, is all north lights, and Kensington may be reckoned a sort of orgie or debauch of studios. Paint is in the air wherever you turn; the very thoroughfares, as witness the Abbey Road, are named after distinguished brethren of the brush. The lower classes of the population devote themselves to what one may term the menial service of gentlemen who paint, the males being all picture-packers and van-drivers, and the females and infants all artists' models.

And, truth to tell, not only do you, the great and the eminent, and the choice-souled palette-wafflers, dwell in the suburbs, but you are of the suburbs, suburban. Consciously or unconsciously, you paint inevitably, not for posterity, but for Suburbia. Even if your pictures fetch a thousand pounds per picture, frame included, your fame and emolument are really suburban matters. Your picture gets hung in an odd corner of a dull-witted plutocrat's palace. Some day the plutocrat dines and wines a gentleman with an eye to the mainest of chances. He stumbles by accident on your immortal work, points out to Pluto that it would engrave admirably, and the thing is done. All Suburbia rushes to pay half a guinea a time for you, and your name creeps into paragraphs and the art criticisms of the *Times* newspaper. You can no more help painting for Suburbia, consciously or unconsciously, than you can help breathing the circumambient air.

It were idle for me to adjure you to give it up—to implore that you should retire out of Suburbia into the winds and the rains and the bits of sunshine, there to chew the ends of your beard and produce something which the Royal Academy and the reproducers would spurn with objurgation and malediction. Go ahead for all you are worth, gather the rosebuds while you may, paint the portraits of the gilded suburb and his pea-flour-fed wife airily and magnificently. When you see one little boy helping another little boy with a crutch across a street, go home and put three months into it, and call it 'Bear ye one another's Burdens.' For by these shifts you shall get R.A. after your name, and purchase what remains of the lease of the house of a dead and bankrupt ornament of your profession, and live yourself lavishly, with wine to your dinner every night and clean shirts of a morning, and die full of bread and honour, and leave enough money for your sons 'to conduct themselves like gentlemen' in a feeble and undistinguished way till they, too, die and pass.

I do not wish to frighten you, my dear Mr. Subub, A.R.A., R.A., R.I.W.C., R.I.P., or otherwise; but when it comes to a certain improbable hour in the history of this universe, I would rather be even one of the administrators of the Chantrey Bequest than your own fat, greasy, designing, canvas-walloping self.

CHAPTER XXI

CHEAP CLASSICS

I SUPPOSE that the latest outbreak of literary vulgarity is largely a matter of Suburbia. I say literary vulgarity, but on the whole, perhaps, the fault is not so much literary as commercial, though the critics have had something to do with it. For quite ten years past those shining ornaments of commerce, the publishing and book-selling trades, have been industriously bent upon the great work of cheapening themselves out of existence. It would be invidious to suggest who started the merry game. Possibly it was the booksellers, possibly it was the publishers. In any case, some genius who was either a bookseller or a publisher came to the conclusion that if books could only be properly cheapened somebody would make a fortune. Therefore, before the book-buying world there suddenly began to appear, in all sorts of specious covers, all manner of books at the marvellous price of twelve pence!

Of course they had to be for the most part out-of-copyright books, or the thing could not have been done. Out-of-copyright books do not involve the horrible duty of royalty-paying, such moneys as they may bring in being thus available for division among the pure traders. And a good name for out-of-copyright books, need one say, is 'classics.' I do not think it is far wide of the mark to assert that the first series of cheap classics put upon the market during the latter eighties did produce a fair amount of money for somebody. And very speedily cheap classics became a really important line for booksellers and publishers alike. Competition brought her sharp tooth into the business with her usual alacrity, and over classics the cheerful tradesmen who call books 'goods' have been cutting one another's throats ever since.

Cheap Classics

From time to time people who 'really know' fall to writing pretty articles on the subject, and they assure us with great satisfaction and much licking of the lips that the 'late demand for classics has been nothing short of astounding,' and that many thousands of pounds must have come into certain coffers accordingly. It is obvious, however, that cheapness in this direction is not exactly an undiluted advantage. Like many another piece of enterprise, it has already begun to retort upon its originators. For, at the time of writing, the book-marts, wholesale and retail, simply groan with cheap goods, and the persons who, in the nature of things, ought to be handing out books at five shillings, and upwards, do little else but scurry round for the nimble ninepence, or at best the nimbler one-and-a-penny-halfpenny.

The book-market, we are told, has been glutted ever since—well, before the South African War. There are too many publishers, and the majority of them produce too many books. This may be the truth. But it is certain that the cheap classic boom has been one of the principal causes of the glut. There are people in the world who approve of the whole proceeding. They argue that publishing and bookselling are of no importance as opposed to the spread of the light. Shakespeare, Milton, Bacon, Dryden, Pope, Burns, Coleridge, Wordsworth, Keats, Byron, Hazlitt, out-of-copyright Tennyson, and out-of-copyright Browning, with a top-dressing of Marcus Aurelius, Omar Khayyám, and Epictetus, are the light, and the sale of them in hundreds of thousands, and for next to nothing, is good for the world. Who shall peruse his contemporaries if he can lay hands on the masters for a mere song? In theory nothing could be nobler; in point of fact nothing could be stupider.

The rush for low-priced classics has been a mean, discreditable suburban rush, if ever there was one. It is Suburbia that purchases these grisly books, and Suburbia alone. Show me a house with its rows of skimpily-bound, undersized shilling or eighteen-penny volumes, and I will show you a house in which the spirit of

Dalston and Clapham and Surbiton and Crouch End rules supreme.

It is commonly set down to the credit and glory of cheap classics that their introduction has brought 'what is best in the literatures of the world' within reach of the poorest. The volumes are believed by the foolish to be acquired by starving and eager students, penurious persons of culture, the poor but honest lower classes, genius just escaped from the Board Schools, and so on and so forth. The facts, however, are quite otherwise. Indeed, it is questionable whether the kind of persons indicated constitute even so much as ten per cent. of the great army of cheap classic buyers.

Probably without knowing what he did, a prominent manufacturer of cheap classics lately hit the right nail on the head by advertising his wares under the caption of 'Books as Furniture.' This, in a phrase, has always been the suburban idea of books, and always will be. It belongs to the same scheme of things as the early Victorian fashion of setting half a dozen choice volumes in cloth gilt round a loo-table for show, and for show only. Nobody read those volumes, and I am seriously disposed to the opinion that nobody reads the cloth and lambskin atrocities which are their successors.

The cynics to a man have had their fling at the bucolic and uncultivated owner of lands who orders his library from some furniture-dealer by the lineal yard. We have heard of this fellow over and over again, and, it is to be presumed, laughed at him. The suburban person with a library, however, is no laughing matter, being, indeed, rather an object for tears. The rich uncultivated man buys a library which he does not propose to read, because he knows that the great houses of his fellows contain fine libraries, and some of them have become famous thereby. The suburban library-purchaser, on the other hand, has taken to book-buying simply and solely because the books are cheap and fit most sweetly into dainty bookcases, book-troughs, corner book-shelves, and the like. Indeed, the libraries of Suburbia are to all intents on a footing with the parlours of Suburbia—that is to say, they have their basis in Suburbia's raging desire to make an extravagant show out of the least possible money. That Shakespeare and Milton, to say nothing of the rest of the masters, should be put to such base uses—degraded, as it were, to the ungodly purpose of decking out the bright little home of Mr. Subub—seems to me ten thousand pities.

There cannot be the slightest doubt that, if the Suburbans did in fact read the classics which they purchase with such avidity, the said classics would do them a great amount of good. Nobody who has the smallest respect for letters will argue that even an entire neglect of contemporary writing in favour of the classics would not be beneficial to the suburbans. But the bare fact that the acquisition of classics has in a great measure rendered Suburbia apathetic towards the literary output of the day proves that Suburbia does not read what it buys. For the person who is properly read there can be no such thing as standing still. The world moves, and with it there is steady progression for better or for worse. The literature of the moment may be decadent and inept and trifling, but the cultivated person will make himself sufficiently acquainted with it, inasmuch as he is a cultivated person.

Shakespeare is for all time, and so are sundry others, but none of them makes really for the exclusion of what shall come after them. Rather may they be likened to large whetters of the appetite, or established standards which point the literary road through the future. If there be anything at all in the scheme of the universe, if we are to believe that knowledge grows from more to more, that every age is the heir of the age that went before it, it is incumbent upon us to believe that there are still chances for literature. It is childish to assume that poetry, let us say, came to an end with Tennyson, or that fiction came to an end with Thackeray. It is equally childish to assume that the supremeness of Homer and Dante and Shakespeare is ultimate. A man who had known the 'Iliad' and the 'Odyssey' for great literature in the years immediately anterior to the appearance of the 'Inferno' might have believed in his heart that Homer was the highest word in poetry, and that the next word were an impossibility. And so the inheritor of Homer and Dante both might, while yet there was no Shakespeare, have believed that there never could be peer for these poets. And yet we have now Shakespeare. And some day, without a doubt, the world will have somebody who can range by prescriptive right with all three of them. And as that great somebody is sure to have advent—that is to say, of course, if the planet does not cease to exist beforehand—it is natural that people of a literary leaning should keep a sharp look-out for him. And it is natural, too, that they should keep a close eye on lesser men, inasmuch as it is out of lesser men that the bigger ones, philosophically speaking, take root. In other words, the greatest authors do not obtain their inspiration, and least of all their material, out of great authors. It is the myriads of little authors who feed, sustain, and nurture the huger ones. Obviously, therefore, no man of parts can afford to indulge the suburban habit of neglect of his contemporaries.

At an hour when two of the leading publishing houses are flooding the country with sixpenny classics—I charge and implore you to think of sixpenny!—it seems ungracious to suggest that cheapness in books is a wicked, undesirable, and damnable thing. But the fact remains. Over those sixpenny classics the vast armies of suburban persons who omitted to cover their walls with classics at a shilling will grin and gloat and rub thrifty knuckles, and say, 'Is it not plain that everything comes to him who waits?' Behold, for the approved literary furnishings obtained by Smith at the arduous price of a shilling the volume, I, Brown, who had the shrewdness to hold for a season my money, pay but sixpence.' And Jones will infallibly come on at threepence; and I make no doubt that on the day before the blasts of Heaven are blown upon this footstool some Scotch publishing firm or other will rush obscenely out with a whole Shakespeare for three-halfpence, and a free Rabelais thrown in with each copy. In that day Suburbia shall come sweetly into its literary own, and the devil shall take the hindmost, or, as it were, the least costly.

CHAPTER XXII

THE FUTURE

And now, when all things are said, what is going to happen to us, where shall we be a century hence, what is our ultimate destiny, and what are our conclusions, if any? I do not think that anyone capable of putting two and two together can fail of a sufficient answer to these questions, that is to say, so far as it is humanly possible to forecast what has not yet actually [illegible].

[illegible] things suburban, so far as they [illegible] immediate future at any rate, is [illegible] by certain proposals which have [illegible] for the organization and [illegible] an entirely new suburb. Here is [illegible] of these proposals, which I shall commend to the reader's attention, both because of the facts it contains and the admirably suburban and complacent tone in which it is written:

'With the object of setting up an ideal suburb within a twopenny fare of the City, the option to purchase 240 acres on the borders of Hampstead Heath has been obtained by Earl Grey, the Earl of Crewe, the Bishop of London, Sir John Gorst, Sir A. Robert Hunter, Sir Walter Hazell, Mr. Herbert Marnham, and Mrs. S. A. Barnett. These form the "Garden Suburban Trust," and already they have mapped out a complete scheme and have plans drawn up for the proposed suburban Utopia. . . . The land embraces, on three sides, the eighty acres soon to be added to Hampstead Heath. The narrow strip north and south of this space is for the erection of large houses. At the western end the middle and professional classes will live in houses commanding a view of the open space and the pine-trees on the hill.' We are told, further, that in the extreme west of the property there will be 'an industrial quarter with rents down to seven and sixpence per week,' and that this quarter will be 'so laid out that every cottage catches the rays of the setting sun in its pretty bay-windows.' Also, 'the Utopian idea will be further realized in the delightful quarters designed for single women—typists and the like—who will have charming rooms leading out to tennis-courts. Single men will be lodged in similar quarters.' It is notable, too, that the rents will be 'at the ordinary market rate,' and that the venture 'has got to pay a dividend.' Two hundred and fifty thousand pounds are asked for wherewithal to carry out the scheme. The author of the idea is Mrs. Barnett, the wife of Canon Barnett, 'and at the Warden's Lodge, Toynbee Hall, several hundreds of applications for houses and promises of support have already been received.'

Now, with every respect to Mrs. Barnett, the question arises, Is this a step in the right direction? To my way of thinking it is not. It is a suburban step, certainly—a projection and carrying forward of the true suburban ideal. But that it is a

specious, vulgar, and undesirable movement cannot, in my opinion, be doubted. Any movement that proposes to hand over to Suburbia the things that it is wont to express the keenest and most anxious desire for, is a movement to be deprecated. One can well understand that Mrs. Barnett has already been inundated with 'applications for houses and promises for support'; for are not Earl Grey, the Earl of Crewe, and the Bishop of London, to say nothing of Sir John Gorst and Sir Robert Hunter, interested in the concern?

Here, indeed, you have precisely the bait that Suburbia could no more leave untasted than hungry trout can resist the skilfully tied artificial fly. For what does this combination represent? Why, it represents in one fell swoop, as it were, dignity, good blood, probity, substantiality, and security of investment, which, of course, is precisely what the investing suburban invariably runs after.

Then, again, the houses of the middle and professional classes are to be erected in 'the

western end of the estate.' How appropriate and how genteel! And every cottage, even though it be meanly and squalidly 'down to seven and sixpence per week,' will nevertheless 'catch the rays of the sun in its pretty bay-windows.' That touch will be worth a great many applications for houses and a great many promises of support in itself. It is just the sort of sentimental, and withal meaningless and illusive, touch which can be calculated to carry Suburbia and the altruists clean off their legs; while as to the typists and the like, who will have 'charming rooms leading out on to tennis-courts,' what could be more entirely and exquisitely to the suburban mind?

From beginning to end the scheme is as suburbany as mortal scheme could well be. That it will succeed, as schemes nowadays go, I do not doubt. Nobody will lose money over it, and the dividend which 'has got' to be paid will in all probability be forthcoming to the uttermost farthing. But you shall go twenty years hence to gaze upon your Utopia with lack-lustre eye and moralize.

It is impossible for combinations of persons to save the soul of Suburbia by pandering to its stupid material aspirations. This is where the philanthropists, and the reformers, and the philosophers of our time go completely and pathetically wrong. Before you can ring in the true, you must ring out the false; and if your true is a mere projection of, and improvement upon, your false, it is still false and rotten, and will be so for all time.

If Suburbia is to work out a salvation for itself, it will have to do so by devolution rather than evolution, by retrogression rather than progression. If, on the other hand, it is to continue logically on its present lines, it will come inevitably to the following preposterous passes: For political guidance it shall look to a glorified John Burns, backed up by a fluttering, abject, renunciatory committee of Countesses of Warwick; its spiritual authorities shall be hustlers of the type of the Rev. R. J. Campbell and the Bishop of London, men who will always contrive to be too busy for sainthood; for authors it shall have Mr. J. K. Jerome to make it guffaw, Dr. Barrie to make it simper and snivel, and Mr. H. G. Wells to make it idiotically sure of itself; it shall go clothed upon with the attire of Mr. George Bernard Shaw; its music shall be an affair of pure gramophone; its arts shall be of the camera, mechanically coloured; its newspapers shall be five a penny and sillier than the Harmsworth publications; and it shall do its journeyings gratis in State-supported twopenny tubes. It will become as hard and as metallic and as unemotional as solid brass; the dwindling soul of it shall die out utterly and be extinguished, and it shall put its trust in foul socialism and the most villainous materialism. Heaven save us from being there to see!

NOTE

SINCE the ultimate chapter of this work got itself into type there has been published by that ancient and Dickensiated house, Messrs. Chapman and Hall, a pretentious sociological essay entitled 'A Modern Utopia.' The author, Mr. H. G. Wells, is no doubt an exceedingly worthy young man, inasmuch as he has achieved 'first-class honours in *Zoology*.' All the same, if there be any virtue in the written word, and if Suburbia be a force against which honest people must struggle, one is compelled to consider Mr. Wells in the light of an enemy to society. Being himself of a temperament which is purely suburban, and of a suburban way of thought, it is natural that he should chance upon suburban ruts and plod therein suburbanly. He made his reputation, such as it is, out of a thrice suburbanized science, blown up and eked out with a mechanical suburban imagination. For years Mr. Wells has been 'delighting' countless thousands of suburbans with a formula which suggests in effect that it is not imaginatively impossible for a man to develop a glass cuticle or a woman talking-apparatus all round her head. With fancies of this nature Mr. Wells has repeatedly ravished the readers of *Pearson's Magazine* and similar organs of culture, which readers are suburban to a soul. And having waxed rich, as suburban riches go, out of these contributions to English letters, Mr. Wells would fain try his hand at prettier game.

But he is holden by the cords of his suburbanism, and though he may be quite unconscious of the circumstance, the trail of that suburbanism glisters slimily over every page of his high-pitched sociological essays. In 'A Modern Utopia' he professes himself most anxious to curry favour with the learned, and in proof of this anxiety he offers the learned an appendix in the shape of 'A portion of a paper read to the Oxford Philosophical Society,' and subsequently printed in *Mind*. This paper is called clumsily 'Scepticism of the Instrument.' It is designed to announce Mr. Wells's discovery of such philosophical commonplaces as 'a doubt of the objective reality of classification,' and the disposition of mentality 'to accumulate intention in terms.' This kind of thing, of course, will be as new to Suburbia as it appears to have been new to Mr. Wells so recently as November 8, 1903. But the learned have known all about it any time this thousand years, and such learned as happen to be left among us will, if they hear of Mr. Wells's philosophical effort at all, inevitably smile.

But my disgust of Mr. Wells is not altogether concerned with his alleged philosophy. The wickedness of him has really nothing to do with philosophy, though he would have us believe otherwise. In plain terms, it is a simple question of tactics, of approach, of posture. Mr. Wells takes the line of least resistance, and assumes the world as it appears to him to be. Then he calls his South Kensington 'ologies' to his aid, and proceeds to suggest what is going to become of us in the long result. Unluckily, however, the world, as it appears to Mr. Wells, is not the world at all, being, in fact, merely Suburbia, and the 'ologies' of South Kensington have no virtue to make a prophet out of a man whose premises are wrong, and whose aims for all his protestations are traversable.

If Mr. Wells has any vision worth the name, he must be fully aware that a logical progression of the present social system—in essence, an almost entirely suburban social system—does not spell pretty things. Yet, for the ease and comfort and self-satisfaction of Suburbia, Mr. Wells makes a fairly reasonable Utopia out of it. And every one of his fine flowers of resultancy is wired up and tinctured and spread out to encourage greasy Mr. Subub, and to confirm him in the opinion that his future is glorious and assured. Hearken to the prophet:

'The general effect of a Utopian population is vigour. Everyone one meets seems to be not only in good health, but in training; one rarely meets fat people, bald people, or bent or gray.' Again: 'The dress is varied and graceful. That of the women reminds one most of the Italian fifteenth century; they have an abundance of soft and beautifully coloured stuffs, and the clothes even of the poorest fit admirably.' Also 'the doubles of people who are naturally foppish on earth will be foppish in Utopia. . . . Everyone will not be quiet in tone, or harmonious or beautiful.'

Here, of course, we have radiant hints of the sweetest things the suburban heart could desire. 'One rarely meets fat people, bald people, or bent or gray.' 'The dress of the women reminds one most of the Italian fifteenth century.' 'Everyone will not be quiet in tone, or harmonious or beautiful.' 'Oh, that will be glory for me,' warbles

Mr. Subub at the bare notion of such proposals, and I am afraid that Mr. Wells intends that Subub should so warble.

The instances of rank suburbanism contained in 'A Modern Utopia' are well-nigh infinite. Everything is arranged to work out in precisely the way the London County Council could wish it to work out.

I append a day-dream for donkeys which the L.C.C. will approve as an ass approves thistles :

'One will come into this place as one comes into a noble mansion. They will have flung great arches and domes of glass above the wider spaces of the town; the slender beauty of the perfect metal-work far overhead will be softened to a fairy-like unsubstantiality by the mild London air. It will be the London air we know, clear of filth and all impurity—that same air that gives our October days their unspeakable clarity, and makes London twilight mysteriously beautiful. We shall go along avenues of architecture that will be emancipated from the last memories of the squat temple boxes of the Greek, the buxom curvatures of Rome; the Goth in us will have taken to steel and countless new materials as kindly as once he took to stone. The gay and swiftly-moving platforms of the public ways will

Crown 8vo., cloth gilt

HIS MASCOT By L. T. MEADE, Author of "Little W Hester," etc.

THE TERROR BY NIGHT By JAMES MACLAR COBBAN, Author of "A Soldier and a Gentleman," etc.

THE HARVEST OF LOVE By C. RANGER-GU Author of "The Serf," "The Hypocrite," etc.

THE OPAL SERPENT By FERGUS HUME, Author "The Mystery of a Hansom Cab," etc.

ALTON OF SOMASCO By HAROLD BINDLOSS, Aut of "The League of the Leopard," etc.

THE REBEL PRINCE By SETH COOK COMSTO Author of "Monsieur le Capitaine Douay." With Photograv Frontispiece from a drawing by HAROLD COPPING.

THE ROOK'S NEST By G. W. APPLETON, Autho "The Mysterious Miss Cass," etc.

JANE SHORE: A Romance of History By J. MUDDOCK, Author of "Sweet 'Doll' of Haddon Hall," etc. W frontispiece of the Heroine, after Bartolozzi's famous picture.

CHILDREN OF EARTH By SIDNEY PATERNOST Author of "Gutter Tragedies," "The Motor Pirate," etc.

A DAUGHTER OF THE MANSE By SA TYTLER, Author of "Citoyenne Jacqueline," etc.

THE TENDERFOOT By W. J. SHEPPARD.

THE SOUL OF A VILLAIN By MRS. HUGHES-GI

JOHN LON

MATILDA, COUNTESS OF TUSCANY

By Mrs. MARY E. HUDDY

Demy 8vo., with 4 magnificent Photogravure Plates, **12s.** *net.*
Second Revised Edition

The Times (column and a half review) says: "Mrs. Huddy's choice of a subject is a clever one. Until the appearance of the volume now before us, there has not been in England any important study of Matilda, the 'Grande Contessa' of Tuscany. Every history of the Popes or the Middle Ages, every account of Italy in the Eleventh Century, furnishes fragments about her; but there has been no consecutive record of her life. Yet she was one of the most dominant personalities of the Middle Ages, and the greatest woman that they produced."

The Daily News (half a column review) says: "Mrs. Huddy has a fascinating subject in a famous lady. In undertaking the task of writing her life in English, Mrs. Huddy is first in the field. She has told the story in considerable detail, and has covered a wide area. Mrs. Huddy has a great subject. She has attempted to leave no part of this great drama of history untold. The story is full of interest, and brightened by romantic incident and picturesque description."

The Pall Mall Gazette (half a column review) says: "Matilda was undoubtedly the most lustrous figure in the portrait gallery of her sex in the Latin world of the Middle Ages. She, indeed, played what may be called a decisive part in the governing crisis of mediæval Europe. The story is inherently piquant and possessing, dignified and eventful."

GLIMPSES OF THE AGES

OR,

The "*Superior*" and "Inferior" Races, so-called, Discussed in the Light of *Science* and History

By THEOPHILUS E. SAMUEL SCHOLES, M.D., Etc.

Demy 8vo., **12s.** *net.*

In this work the aim of the author has been to show that, in the three great divisions of mankind, there exists an absolute equality. The kinds of equality considered are physical and mental. The volume deals exhaustively with the much-discussed question of the equality of the coloured races with that of the white, and the author introduces much information of an absorbing nature to prove that the so-called "superiority" of the whites over the coloured races is an untenable theory.

IN OLD NORTHUMBRIA

A Volume of Verse

By R. H. FORSTER, Author of "The Last Foray," "In Steel and Leather," "Strained Allegiance," etc.

Crown 8vo., cloth gilt, **3s. 6d.** *net.* *With 8 Illustrations by* R. C. Reid

JOHN LONG'S CARLTON CLASSICS

Prices Decorative Wrapper, 6d. net; Artistic Cloth, gilt, 6d. net; Leather, gilt gold-blocked back and side, 1s. net. Size, 6 in. by 4 in. by ½ in. It is the aim of this se to present in tasteful and artistic form the World's favourite little masterpieces in prose verse, and the Publisher believes that these Classics will be considered new and distinct and surpass any series at present before the public in the beauty of their printing and daintiness of their format. Each Volume contains a Biographical Introduction by the Edi Mr. HANNAFORD BENNETT. The first twelve works are

CHILDE HAROLD'S PILGRIMAGE	LORD BYRON
MUCH ADO ABOUT NOTHING	SHAKESPEARE
THE FOUR GEORGES	W. M. THACKERAY
WARREN HASTINGS	LORD MACAULAY
TALES (Selected)	EDGAR ALLAN POE
CHRISTABEL, and Other Poems	S. T. COLERIDGE
A SENTIMENTAL JOURNEY	LAURENCE STERNE
THE LIFE OF NELSON (double Vol.)	ROBERT SOUTHEY
THE BLESSED DAMOZEL and Other Poems	DANTE GABRIEL ROSS
ON HEROES AND HERO WORSHIP	THOMAS CARLYLE
SONNETS	SHAKESPEARE
RASSELAS	SAMUEL JOHNSON

THE HAYMARKET NOVELS

A Series of Copyright Novels by Popular Authors. The Volumes are printed up superior Antique Wove Paper, handsomely bound in specially designed cover, red c heavily Gold Blocked at back. The size of the volumes is 7½ in. by 5½ in. by 1¼ in., length from 300 to 350 pages, and the price 2s. 6d. each.

Volumes Now Ready.

FATHER ANTHONY (Illustrated)
A CABINET SECRET (Illustrated)
AN OUTSIDER'S YEAR
FUGITIVE ANNE
THE FUTURE OF PHYLLIS
BENEATH THE VEIL
THE SCARLET SEAL
A DIFFICULT MATTER
A PASSING FANCY
BITTER FRUIT
AN ILL WIND
A WOMAN'S "NO"
MIDSUMMER MADNESS
THE SILENT HOUSE IN PIMLICO
THE CRIMSON CRYPTOGRAM
A TRAITOR IN LONDON
THE MACHINATIONS OF JANET
THE MAGNETIC GIRL
THE BURDEN OF HER YOUTH
IN SUMMER SHADE
A FLIRTATION WITH TRUTH
DELPHINE

SOME RECENT POPULAR NOVELS

Six Shillings each

THE STORM OF LONDON - - F. DICKBERRY
THE MASK - - - - - - - WILLIAM LE QUEUX
BLIND POLICY - - - - - - GEORGE MANVILLE FENN
THE AMBASSADOR'S GLOVE ROBERT MACHRAY
LADY SYLVIA - - - - - - LUCAS CLEEVE
THE WATERS OF OBLIVION ADELINE SERGEANT
THE FATE OF FELIX - - - - - - - MRS. COULSON KERNAHAN
THE BOOK OF ANGELUS DRAYTON - MRS. FRED REYNOLDS
THE TEMPTATION OF ANTHONY ALICE M DIEHL
LITTLE WIFE HESTER - - L. T. MEADE
THE NIGHT OF RECKONING - FRANK BARRETT
ROSAMOND GRANT - - - MRS. LOVETT CAMERON
ORD EVERSLEIGH'S SINS - - - - VIOLET TWEEDALE
CONFESSIONS OF A YOUNG LADY - RICHARD MARSH
LOVE AND TWENTY - - - - JOHN STRANGE WINTER
HIS REVERENCE THE RECTOR - SARAH TYTLER
THE INFORMER - - - - - - FRED WHISHAW
THE FACE IN THE FLASHLIGHT FLORENCE WARDEN
THE WAR OF THE SEXES F. E. YOUNG
COUNT REMINY - - - - - - - JEAN MIDDLEMASS
THE PROVINCIALS - - - - - - LADY HELEN FORBES
STRAINED ALLEGIANCE - - - - - R. H. FORSTER
OLIVE KINSELLA - - - - - - CURTIS YORKE
FROM THE CLUTCH OF THE SEA J. E. MUDDOCK
LORD OF HIMSELF - - - - MRS. AYLMER GOWING
MISS ARNOTT'S MARRIAGE RICHARD MARSH
AN IMPOSSIBLE HUSBAND FLORENCE WARDEN
A WOMAN OF BUSINESS - - - MAJOR ARTHUR GRIFFITHS
THE COUNTESS OF MOUNTENOY JOHN STRANGE WINTER
A SOLDIER AND A GENTLEMAN J. MACLAREN COBBAN
THE ADVENTURES OF MIRANDA L. T. MEADE
HEARTS ARE TRUMPS - - - - - SARAH TYTLER
THE GIRL IN GREY - - - - - - CURTIS YORKE
A FOOL WITH WOMEN - - - - - FRED WHISHAW
THE IDENTITY OF JANE - - - - - ALICE METHLEY
A BOND OF SYMPATHY - - - - - COL. ANDREW HAGGARD
MADEMOISELLE NELLIE - - - - - LUCAS CLEEVE
THE SECRET PASSAGE - - FERGUS HUME
IN SPITE OF THE CZAR (8 Illus.) 5s. GUY BOOTHBY
A BRIDE FROM THE SEA (8 Illus.) 5s. GUY BOOTHBY

"A real triumph of modern publishing."—*Pall Mall Gazette.*

JOHN LONG'S LIBRARY OF MODERN CLASSICS

A series of great works of fiction by modern authors. Not pocket editions, but large, handsome, and fully-illustrated volumes for the bookshelf, printed in large type on the best paper. Biographical Introductions and Photogravure Portraits. Size, 8 in. by 5¼ in.; thickness, 1¼ in. Prices: Cloth gilt, **2s.** net each; Leather, Gold Blocked and Silk Marker, **3s.** net each; or in Half-bound Classic Vellum, **5s.** net each.

Volumes now ready.

THE THREE CLERKS - - - - - - (480 pp.) ANTHONY TROLL
THE CLOISTER AND THE HEARTH - (672 pp.) CHARLES READE
THE WOMAN IN WHITE - - - - - (576 pp.) WILKIE COLLINS
ADAM BEDE - - - - - - - - - - (480 pp.) GEORGE ELIOT
THE HISTORY OF HENRY ESMOND (432 pp.) W. M. THACKERAY
WESTWARD HO! - - - - - - - (600 pp.) CHARLES KINGSLEY
TOM BROWN'S SCHOOLDAYS - - (320 pp.) THOMAS HUGHES

Other Volumes to follow.

"I know of no pleasanter or more tasteful reprints."—*Academy.* "A marvel of cheapness."—*Spectator.* "A marvellous bargain."—*Truth.* "Wonderfully cheap."—*Globe.* "Remarkable in price and format."—*Daily Mail.* "Admirable in print, paper, and binding."—*Saturday Review.*

NEW VOLUMES FOR 1906

THE WORLD MASTERS	GEORGE GRIFFITH
BENEATH THE VEIL	ADELINE SERGEANT
THE BURDEN OF HER YOUTH	L. T. MEADE
LE SELVE	OUIDA
SWEET "DOLL" OF HADDON HALL	J. E. MUDDOCK
THE LADY OF THE ISLAND	GUY BOOTHBY
MIDSUMMER MADNESS	MRS. LOVETT CAME
THE MAGNETIC GIRL	RICHARD MARSH
No. 3, THE SQUARE	FLORENCE WARDEN
THE JADE EYE	FERGUS HUME

THE FOLLOWING ARE NOW READY:

AN OUTSIDER'S YEAR	FLORENCE WARDEN
SOMETHING IN THE CITY	FLORENCE WARDEN
THE LOVELY MRS. PEMBERTON	FLORENCE WARDEN
THE MYSTERY OF DUDLEY HORNE	FLORENCE WARDEN
THE BOHEMIAN GIRLS	FLORENCE WARDEN
KITTY'S ENGAGEMENT	FLORENCE WARDEN
OUR WIDOW	FLORENCE WARDEN
THE TURNPIKE HOUSE	FERGUS HUME
THE GOLDEN WANG-HO	FERGUS HUME
THE SILENT HOUSE IN PIMLICO	FERGUS HUME
THE BISHOP'S SECRET	FERGUS HUME
THE CRIMSON CRYPTOGRAM	FERGUS HUME
A TRAITOR IN LONDON	FERGUS HUME
WOMAN—THE SPHINX	FERGUS HUME
A WOMAN'S "NO"	MRS. LOVETT CAME
A DIFFICULT MATTER	MRS. LOVETT CAME
THE CRAZE OF CHRISTINA	MRS. LOVETT CAME
A PASSING FANCY	MRS. LOVETT CAME
BITTER FRUIT	MRS. LOVETT CAME
AN ILL WIND	MRS. LOVETT CAME
CURIOS; or, The Strange Adventures of Two Bachelors	RICHARD MARSH
MRS. MUSGRAVE AND HER HUSBAND	RICHARD MARSH
ADA VERNHAM, ACTRESS	RICHARD MARSH
THE EYE OF ISTAR	WILLIAM LE QUEU
THE VEILED MAN	WILLIAM LE QUEU
A MAN OF TO-DAY	HELEN MATHERS
THE SIN OF HAGAR	HELEN MATHERS
THE JUGGLER AND THE SOUL	HELEN MATHERS
FATHER ANTHONY	ROBERT BUCHANAN
THE WOOING OF MONICA	L. T. MEADE
THE SIN OF JASPER STANDISH	RITA
A CABINET SECRET	GUY BOOTHBY
THE FUTURE OF PHYLLIS	ADELINE SERGEANT
A BEAUTIFUL REBEL	ERNEST GLANVILLE
THE PROGRESS OF PAULINE KESSLER	FREDERIC CARREL
IN SUMMER SHADE	MARY E. MANN
GEORGE AND SON	EDWARD H. COOPE
THE SCARLET SEAL	DICK DONOVAN
THE THREE DAYS' TERROR	J. S. FLETCHER

☞ *Other Novels by the most popular Authors of the day will be added to the Ser from time to time.*

Lightning Source UK Ltd.
Milton Keynes UK
UKOW06f2352281117
313528UK00012BC/853/P

9 781333 994655